Betrayed

Betrayed

PETER J. FALOTICO

CHAPTER 1

T̲HE BANK MANAGER'S FOOT FIRMLY planted on the silent alarm button on the floor, the three holdup men fled Worthington Citizens Bank none the wiser, carrying sacks of stolen money. Police responded to the alarm immediately, their sirens growing louder with each passing second. Already, roadblocks cordoned off main arteries and secondary roads from any hope of escape, even before the robbers could make it to the getaway vehicle.

"Go! Go!" the last one in yelled, slamming the door on his foot and then shutting it hurriedly as the wheelman peeled out under maximum engine rpm.

The getaway car narrowly missed a police squad car with siren at full pitch, red lights flashing, which had fishtailed through the intersection. "Faster, you moron! Faster!" the leader screamed to the driver, who did as he was told and maneuvered a hard right down a narrow alleyway known (to the leader) as a way to bypass the main highway out of town.

When planning the escape, the holdup men had failed to consider the possibility of roadblocks jamming the roads leading out of town before they could get clear of the area. At the end of the narrow alleyway, two squad cars blocked off any chance of leaving town around the aqueduct, and the driver slammed on the brakes and spun the vehicle around.

The trio drove around in circles in a futile attempt to avoid the police. They were cornered into a bloody shootout at a construction site when they pulled up behind an embankment, burst out of the car, and fired at policemen as they ran. The well-trained officers played hardball, caught the robbers in the crossfire, and killed the thieves in a matter of minutes. Bullet-riddled bodies lay in silence. Blood pooled on the ground. This was yet another failed attempt to rob the Worthington Citizens Bank. When the press arrived, the arteries and three secondary roads had been shut off within sixty seconds; every available police unit had arrived at their predetermined positions, according to drill, and in record time. The police officers were not shy about their accomplishment.

*　　*　　*

The next day in the exercise yard at the Illinois State Penitentiary in Joliet, inmate John Reed was holding court with newspaper in hand, reporting the story of the botched attempted bank robbery.

John turned to the other cons and said, "Poor planning! Poor friggin' planning! A bunch of amateurs; they bungled what should have been an easy heist."

An inmate too old to fear John asked him, "What makes you think you could have done a better job, Johnny?" The old guy grinned. There fell immediate silence, as the inmates stared at John, fearful that he would turn hostile. They knew what harm John was capable of doing when provoked.

John turned to the old guy, smiled, and said, "I'll show you when I get out of this hole in nine months, old man. All I need are the blueprints of that bank, and I'll show you what I can do."

Another inmate standing by told John, "For a hundred bucks, I could arrange to get you the set of blueprints."

"Set it up," John told him. "I'll have the hundred clams ready." The inmate agreed but warned John that, as the paper stated, Worthington Citizens would be too tough to crack. John smiled arrogantly and said, "Any bank could be broken into by the right expert, and I'm that expert." Yet after paying the hundred dollars for the bank plans, the cocky and brazen John Reed didn't take the time to study them.

*   *   *

John Reed was good-looking. Females he met swooned over him in spite of his Jekyll-Hyde personality: personable one moment, capable of inflicting bodily harm the next. Case in point: John busted the jaw of one inmate just for causing him to spill milk on his uniform while preparing his breakfast cereal. He assaulted another for taking a cigarette without asking, which netted him three weeks in solitary confinement on each count. John, a born leader, backed down from no one.

Strange as it may seem, he loved opera music. A high school dropout, John had fallen in with a gang of young felons who thought that crime was easier than making an honest living, and he had eventually landed in prison for three years for armed robbery. That sentence was to end in nine months. John was about to begin his plan of breaking into the Worthington Bank, just to prove to all the cons that he could pull off what his peers could not.

*   *   *

In spring, nine months later, John was cruising the town of Worthington in his rented Pontiac. He wanted to see the so-called impossible-to-rob Worthington Citizens Bank and to look for temporary living quarters. After circling the bank for the third time, he stopped in the Appliance store adjacent to the bank where the break-in was to take place. *A piece of cake*, John Reed thought to himself. A short drive later, he spotted the Starlight Motel situated only two miles south of Worthington.

He surveyed the motel lobby as he stood at the registration desk. He paid for a room with double-beds for three nights.

He began unpacking his suitcases, first selecting the suitcase with a secret compartment containing the seed money required to finance the heist. John knew that Marty, Hank, and Hal had no money, so all three had agreed that he get an extra ten percent of the take. The hidden funds totaled fifteen thousand dollars. It was the last of the stolen money he had stashed away for such an occasion. He put the money back in its hiding place and finished unpacking. Afterward he lay on the bed to test it. He placed his hands behind his head. He stared at the ceiling and fell asleep.

Screeching automobile tires on the avenue interrupted his nap. It was just as well, since he had to contact Hank, who should have been waiting for his phone call. He left his room in search of a public phone. He found one located in the lobby. He dialed Hank's number.

Hank answered the phone in a low voice. "Yeah, who's this?"

"Hank, you lug head!" John said laughing. "I'm here in Worthington. Grab a pen and paper and jot down the address I'm about to give you."

"Sure, John," Hank answered as he reached for pen and paper. "Okay, John, shoot."

"The Starlight Motel on route 80 two miles south of Worthington. Get a hold of Marty and Hal and head on out. I'll be waiting for you. Oh, and one more thing, Hank. Don't forget the tools for the break-in."

"Sure. Sure. Gotcha covered."

Hank Strauss, fifty-five, looked much older than John. He had a humped back and was the opposite of John as far as attractiveness was concerned. But after meeting him in prison, John had earned Hank's eternal gratitude by taking him under his wing and protecting him from the taunts of the other cons.

*   *   *

Sitting at the bar in the motel lounge sipping a drink, John waited for his three accomplices to show up. When they did, he greeted Hank and Hal with a shaking of hands. He and Marty embraced. "John, you son of a bitch, you look great," Marty said with a smile. "Looks like they took good care of you up the river."

"Sure. They took care of me all right, up the ass," John answered.

John gave Marty money to register in the motel for three days. He and Hal would share the same room. "There's a diner five blocks south of Oaks Street called Ben's. Perfect for meetings. We'll meet there tonight at seven. It's important not to be seen together here at the motel for the next three day's." He reached into his coat pocket and took out a copy of the bank plan. He handed it to Marty with instructions that he and Hal go over it and give him their input and recommendations.

*   *   *

Marty Gibbs, a man of forty, had straight receding black hair. He had a tendency to be too mouthy, which caused him to get into many scrapes with other cons and prison guards. His time in prison was not a total waste because he was trained and had developed into a master auto mechanic. He could have made an honest living and a lucrative one at that. Instead, he had chosen the only profession he wanted: thievery.

Marty nodded and said, "See you tonight at seven, John."

John helped Hank with his bags and they went to their room.

*   *   *

Ben's Diner was a small neighborhood eatery. It wasn't the finest place in town, but it provided the privacy John required for conducting his meeting with the guys.

Hal and Marty were seated at the counter sipping beer when John and Hank arrived. John chose a table at the rear of the diner. He ordered beer for Hank and himself. While they were sipping their drinks, the waitress appeared to announce the dinner specials. She wore a white blouse with a nametag that read "Kay." Her tight-fitting, short, black skirt highlighted her shapely legs. She appeared to be in her early thirties and was maybe five foot seven, 110 pounds. Her long brunette tresses bounced on her shoulders when she walked.

Marty took an immediate shine to her, as he looked her up and down. As he focused his gaze on her shapely legs, his face screamed "horny." He ordered first. "I'll have the hot roast beef sandwich, and you, honey."

"Bug off, buster," the waitress shot back.

John quickly intervened and told the waitress, "Make that the same for all of us."

The waitress thanked John and gave him a sidelong glance as she walked way.

John noticed Marty's eyes following her as she went to the kitchen. John, upset, turned to Marty. "What the hell are you trying to do, screw things up before we get started?"

Marty grinned and said, "Just having fun, John. I wouldn't mind giving her a shot though."

"You know as well as I do that we must keep a low profile during the heist, and that's not the way. As of now, broads are out until the heist is completed. Is that understood?" John looked at all three.

Marty and Hank nodded their heads. Hal hesitated, looked hard and long at Marty, and then shook his head.

*   *   *

Hal Grimes was a young man of twenty-three; he was six-foot one with blonde hair and blue eyes, and he weighed somewhere around 175 pounds. Hal could have had a great future as a commercial artist, but he had dropped out of college in his second year. He did not have the patience to study. He wanted quick, easy money, so he had chosen a life of crime. Eventually, the law caught up with him, and he landed in prison for two years. John had promised him big times when he was released.

*   *   *

"Okay, listen up," John told them. "I drove by the bank three times today. What I saw was a bank that we should have no problem taking. Now here's my plan for the break-in: to begin with, there's an appliance store next to the bank. I walked through the store to see if there was a basement, which there is. The store closes every night at six. That's how we'll gain entrance to the bank: by breaking though the basement wall."

John turned to Hal and said, "At 5:30 on the night of the heist, you will enter the store and pretend to be browsing. Soon as you get the opportunity you slip down to the basement and wait. After the store closes, you let us in the back door. We go to the basement. We do our thing. We leave the same way."

"Break in that early in evening?" Marty asked. "Heavy traffic and all?"

John grinned at Marty and said, "That's the point, Marty. The more traffic, the more noise to cover the jackhammer. If we did it in the middle of the night, the jackhammer would be heard all over the area." John grinned again.

"Hal and me will check out the appliance store basement in the morning. I want to make certain that we brought the proper tools. If everything goes according to plan, the break-in should go down in three days."

John pulled a pack of Marlboros from his pocket. He lit one and dropped the match on the floor. He turned to Marty and asked, "Did you have time to go over the bank plans?"

Marty looked at John and said, "I did," placing the plan on the table.

"Good," John smiled. "Let's have your recommendation."

"Your plan is great but that bank looks awfully tough."

"What the hell are you telling me, Marty? It's just an ordinary bank, ain't it?" John asked, trying to keep his voice down.

"Hey. You asked for my friggin opinion and I gave it to you."

Hal, who felt that things were about to get out of hand, cautiously intervened. "It looks like an ordinary bank, John, but it's a specially constructed building with reinforced steel and concrete, at least two-foot deep, on all four sides." Hal said, running his finger in and around the blueprint. "It would take blasting besides drilling, which would be time consuming, not to mention the noise it would create, which could possibly damage the store and draw the cops." He looked nervously into John's eyes as he spoke.

John suddenly felt stupid and embarrassed. Because of his cocky attitude, he had failed to take the time to study the bank plan. John wanted to hide his embarrassment and said, "Okay, okay. Like I said, Hal and me will check it out in the morning and see if it's as tough as you make it out to be. If it is as tough as you guys say, then I have one other option. If that doesn't work then I'll use 'Plan B.'" John was lying. There wasn't a plan "B."

*   *   *

When he arrived at the appliance store, John turned to Hal and told him, "Keep the salesperson occupied while I sneak down the basement and look around." Hal nodded as they entered. The store was crowded and only one salesman was working. Hal approached the salesman who was already busy with a customer. John opened the basement door and scampered down the steps to begin his inspection. He was shocked to learn that Hal was totally correct; the walls were solid concrete and wired. He kneeled on one knee, running his hand on the floor and thinking that maybe it would be possible to tunnel below the wall line. Blasting was a possibility, but then blasting could be hazardous. He looked at his watch and realized that he had been there long enough. After retreating up the stairs he peeked around and then walked to where Hal was standing. He tapped him on the shoulder, and they walked slowly out of the store unnoticed. For a second time John was upset with himself for not personally checking all the alternatives before making a rash decision to rob the Worthington bank. He turned to Hal and said, "You were correct, Hal. It's a fortress all right. I want to check the plan and the bank one more time before I use my other option."

Hal didn't dare comment. John dropped Hal off at the motel and told him to relax the rest of the day. "You got it, John," Hal answered.

Arriving at his room, John immediately searched for and found a copy of the bank plans in his coat pocket. Sitting on the bed using a pencil as a pointer, he began checking the foundation. "Shit. It's too deep; no way I can tunnel below the line. Blasting would do it; however, it would be dangerous." Infuriated, he tore the plan to shreds and flushed it down the commode. "That takes care of using the basement." Having sworn to everyone that he was going to successfully rob the Worthington bank, he could not now back out of this caper.

He gathered the guys to his room and ordered coffee. "Okay, listen up," he began saying in a low voice. "The break-in through the store basement is out. It's as tough as you guys said it was, so my next option is breaking into the bank by cutting through the roof after midnight. We can get to the roof of the bank using the appliance store building because it has two landings to the roof. Marty, Hal, and me will use ropes to lower us to the bank floor. Hank will stay on the roof. He'll be the lookout and hand us the tools using a rope and a basket. The tools we brought along should be enough to break through the vault. Job done, we leave the same way as we came in." The guys seemed to like the idea and nodded their approval.

John continued, "Don't get too excited yet. I still have to go to the bank and check out the feasibility of breaking in through the roof." John paused and took a sip of coffee, which by this time was lukewarm. "Relax for the rest of the day, I'll check out the bank first thing in morning."

*   *   *

John arrived at the bank just past nine. He was surprised to find a substantial throng of people there. He went to the counter that stored transaction slips. He began filling out deposit slips as he surveyed the ceiling. It was finished with dropped ceiling tiles. There were fluorescent lighting fixtures throughout. John didn't have a clue as to how it was constructed or even wired, so he looked for the guard who happened to be sitting on a stool eyeballing the young women. John walked slowly to where he was sitting and managed to strike up a conversation with him, first talking about the weather and then turning his attention to the bank.

"You have a well-constructed building here, Luke," John said, looking at the guard's nametag.

"Yes, sir; they don't make buildings like this any more."

John pointed to the roof and asked, "Is the roof constructed as well as the rest of the building?"

"No sir!" Luke answered. "The roof is built much stronger with steel I beams encased in concrete and set one foot apart." Luke grinned. John swallowed hard. He immediately realized that breaking through the roof was out, and his final option was dead.

"Wow! I'm impressed," John said as he thanked him and left. Sitting in his car he stared into space. *Well stupid you're out of options. You'd better sit your ass down and come up with your so-called plan B, or risk losing your pride not only with the men but with your inmate friends at the prison to whom you bragged about how easy it was going to be to crash the bank.*

He was horribly upset with himself. However, he was smart enough to realize that whatever plan he came up with would require time; how much he hadn't a clue. Working out of the motel wasn't private enough, and furthermore it was expensive. Unfortunately, his seed money was limited. He started the car and was off to look for a place to live for the duration.

*   *   *

A short drive later John spotted a three-story brick home with a red and white placard neatly placed in the window: "ROOM FOR RENT." John stopped the car, walked up the stone steps, and knocked on the door. Waiting made John irritable. He pulled a pack of Marlboros from his shirt pocket, lit one, and dropped the match on the pavement. "Ah, finally," John exhaled, and tossed the cigarette to the sidewalk. The front door was opened a crack. John could just about see a woman's nose.

"Can I help you young man?" asked the woman, as she gave John the once-over.

John, dressed in his finest attire, smiled and said, "Yes, ma'am, thank you. I'm asking about the room you have for rent."

She opened the door half way, still appearing skeptical and leaning against the door as though ready to slam it shut. Again she looked at John from head to toe. John assumed that she was being cautious, so he flashed a broad smile to help her relax. Concerned about renting the apartment, but mostly thinking about the money, she opened the door all the way and invited him in. She was in her mid 60's or maybe older, and her face was marked by deep wrinkles. She apologized for taking so long to answer his knock, saying something about feeding her cat, and led him to the living room. John looked around the room and, as he suspected, the house was immaculate with every piece of furniture, every lamp, and all the pictures dusted and polished.

"It's a large room, located on the third floor. It has a private bath, and the rent is two hundred dollars a week. The rent includes utilities. One month's payment in advance of course." She continued to ogle John, but now she was smiling.

Without hesitating, John reached into his pocket and pulled out a wad of twenty and one hundred dollar bills. He quickly counted out eight hundred dollars and gave it to her.

Surprised at John's hasty decision to accept the room, she asked, "Are you sure that you don't want to look at the room before deciding?"

"No, thank you." John smiled. "I'm sure that it will be fine."

She excused herself, went to a small desk in the living room, and withdrew a folder containing rental and receipt forms. With her pen in hand, she returned to John and asked his name so that she could make out his receipt of payment.

"Bob London. Er, Robert London," John lied as he stared at the plain, unpretentious, antique-filled room across the hall.

"Yes, Mr. London it is." She completed and handed him the receipt. After handing John the keys, she looked at him again and said, "Mr. London. My, that's an interesting name. Are you from this area?"

"No. California," John replied.

"You're very far from home, aren't you? Here on business? If so, what kind of business are you in?" she asked all in one breath.

Bored by the third degree, feeling his temper rise, he took a mental step backwards, smiled, and quietly murmured, "I'm in the automobile repair business, and my friends and I are opening a shop in the city."

"Oh, a businessman. How nice," she said. "I wish you luck." She thanked John and retreated to the back of the house.

"Thanks, you old bitch," John grumbled to himself as he went up to his room.

He placed his luggage on the floor by the bed and glanced around the room. Just as he suspected, the room was immaculate and fully furnished; in addition to the bed, there were two cozy overstuffed chairs upholstered in an old print. They faced each other with a round table between them. At the far end of the room was a studio couch, likely converted into a bed. John immediately decided it would be perfect for Hank since he would be his roommate for the duration.

*   *   *

Arriving at the motel, John found the guys sitting in the lounge. He got their attention and signaled them, and they followed him to his room. "Okay, this is what we have, after checking the bank and speaking with the guard, the roof is just as tough as the basement, and that leaves me with plan B. However my plan will take more time . . . . "

"How much time?" Marty asked.

"It depends on what additional information I'll need to complete my plan. In the meantime, I rented a room that Hank and me will share for the duration. I noticed a rental sign tacked up side of this house on Sycamore Street, ten blocks south. You guys can work out the rental. If the room doesn't pan out, you can stay here for the night, then look for a room in the morning. Oh and one more item, explain to the landlord that it would have to be a monthly lease so that you can check out at any time. The seven o'clock meeting at

Ben's is still a go." Marty looked at Hal, Hal looked at Marty, and both shook their heads and shrugged their shoulders. "Okay, get a move on." John checked out of the motel and he and Hank were off to the rooming house.

"Come in Hank," John said, offering him a chair. "Take the load off your feet, and have a look at our living quarters for the duration." Hank looked around the room, and said, "Ain't much is it?" Apparently Hank was expecting to have his own room.

"It will do just fine. Besides, it's only temporary."

*   *   *

At seven o'clock, John and Hank arrived at Ben's. Hal and Marty were already seated at the same table as the other night. As the guys read the menu, John asked Marty if he had found a place to crash.

"The Sycamore place," Marty answered. "Two bedrooms and a private bath."

Dressed in her sexy outfit, Kay appeared with her check pad in hand to take their order. Marty was about to make a remark but thought better of it as he looked toward John. They placed their orders and Kay disappeared into the kitchen.

"As I said earlier we'll probably be here in the city for awhile, and I don't like operating out of a rooming house. Meeting here day-in-and-day-out could draw suspicion, so I've decided to rent a garage-type building for whatever time it takes to do the job. We'll use it as a control point—" John paused as the waitress returned with their orders. While placing the food on the table, she stared into John's eyes, causing him to spill beer on his shirt. Irritated, John brushed the cold wet brew from his shirt while at the same time trying to control his temper.

"Oh, I'm sorry," the waitress apologized. Satisfied that she had his attention, she smiled again and returned to the kitchen.

"She goes for you John," Hank said with a devilish grin. John ignored Hank's remark and asked, "Where was I?"

Hank reminded him: "Renting a building for the heist."

John continued, "I will rent a building tomorrow for thirty days. I'm sure that you can't rent for less than a month, so I'll need a map of the city to locate strategic areas in and around the city, and a newspaper to check out the real estate section. I'm looking for a garage-type building. Also, I want to be sure that the shop is located in an isolated area. When I locate the right building, we begin "Operation Heist." The guys smiled and continued feeding their faces.

Hank was the first to finish his meal. John turned to Hank and said, "Since you've finished eating, see if you could find a newsstand and pick up the local paper and a city map while we finish our meals." He gave him money. "Get a jump on it."

Hank was back within fifteen minutes. John placed the newspaper and the map on the table.

The waitress returned and stared directly at John and asked, "Desert for anyone?"

"No, thank you. Everything was fine." John requested the check and they left.

*   *   *

After arriving home, John and Hank settled on the floor, where John spread out the newspaper. Hank did the same with the map. After checking the entire rental section in the newspaper, John found three possible locations.

"Okay, Hank, check this one, located on Fourth Street and Grange Avenue?"

"Christ no, John. That's located one block from the police station."

"Ah, balls," he said in disgust. "Okay, how about this location, North and Ridgeway?"

"Bingo!" Hank shouted. "It's at the edge of town and a good distance from the nearest police station."

"Good. We'll check out the property first thing in the morning. Then we can contact the broker listing the property."

CHAPTER 2

John pulled up in front of the huge red brick building situated on a Street that seemed lightly traveled. He liked what he saw. He then drove to the relator's office.

H & R Realty was a small commercial real estate agency located in the center of town. John parked his car a block from the office. As he and Hank walked toward the office, John said, "Now I'll do all the talking."

"Gotcha, John."

A short, slender, well-groomed gentleman greeted them. He was dressed in a dark blue, pinstriped suit, a blue shirt, and a maroon tie. He walked swiftly toward them with his hand extended, revealing manicured fingernails. "Good morning, gentlemen. I'm Mr. Raymond, first half of R & H Realtors. What can I do for you today?" he said peering at them through wire-rimmed glasses.

Something strange about this guy, John thought as he received his weak handshake. "My partner and I are in the auto repair business. We're planning to open a repair shop in town."

"Fine," Raymond said, with a twinkle in his eye. "Come into my office, please." He led the way.

The natural wood ceiling beams and an oriental carpet impressed John. The cream-colored walls boasted original paintings and objects of art.

Fingering his collar and crossing his legs, first one way then the other, Raymond asked, "In which location are you interested?"

"North and Ridgeway," John replied.

"Yes. I know the property. The location is fabulous for your type of business. In fact, it was once used for the same purpose." Arms folded one over the other, he continued, "If I recall correctly, the equipment is still intact: hydraulic lifts, jacks, and so forth. I can show it to you if you like."

John agreed to see the building, but he told Raymond they would drive in separate cars. Mr. Raymond hastened to his car with attaché' in hand.

The interior of the building was laid out perfectly with an office at the left corner of the entrance. It was furnished with a wooden desk and chair and a gray metal filing cabinet. John perused the building, passing a hydraulic lift and jack stands. Much to John's discomfort, Raymond followed close behind. John turned his head slowly as if looking at the equipment and noticed Raymond watching him intensely. At one point, Raymond stared long and hard into John's eyes, which was a definite attempt to communicate his desires. However, John managed to ignore Raymond's body language and continued looking over the building.

Finally, John said, "This will do just fine. What's the damage?" he asked, forgetting that he was supposed to be an upstanding, educated businessman.

"Damage?" Raymond appeared insulted.

"I'm sorry Mr. Raymond. I meant the rental fee. Also, I prefer a monthly lease. I want to be certain that this is a good location for an auto repair business."

"A monthly lease would be no problem, Mr. . . . . ?"

"Mr. London. Robert London," John answered.

"No problem, Mr. London. If you come to my office this evening at seven, we can discuss all the necessary details including the rental fee," Raymond suggested with a flirting, feminine gesture. He smiled at John, showing his perfectly straight teeth, which were no doubt capped.

He was unquestionably a homosexual. John thought, *I'll be a son-of-a-bitch. This guy has to be gay.* "I appreciate your offer, Mr. Raymond, but I'm a very busy man with much to accomplish in the next few days. I must complete this transaction now or I'll have to look elsewhere."

"Oh, all right then." Mr. Raymond was obviously annoyed. "The cost is eight hundred and fifty dollars a month plus utilities."

"Fine, Mr. Raymond." John reached into the pocket of his trousers, withdrew a roll of bills, peeled off one month's rent, and handed Raymond the money. With his hand extended, palm up, he informed the agent, "I'll take the keys. My partner, Mr. Prew, will return to your office with you to sign the lease. Afterward, would you please drive Mr. Prew home?"

Raymond agreed. Hank, however, wasn't happy about returning to the office with Raymond. But, knowing John . . . .

After Hank and Raymond left, John continued to inspect the shop. His mind was beyond Pluto because he was thinking of the dual job that lay ahead of him when he stumbled upon a huge paint booth, large enough to hold over-sized vehicles. John completed his inspection and locked the door, after which he strolled through the neighborhood making mental notes.

Perfect! John thought. He saw no one in the area except a short, frail elderly woman with white hair walking her Pekinese. Noticeably, there were no children playing in the area.

Enough had been accomplished. John got into his car and sped off.

* * *

As he climbed the front steps of his rooming house, John noticed that the blinds on the first floor window were slightly parted. There she was, the landlady with an eagle eye probably spying on him. John chuckled. He let himself in and trotted up the stairs. As he approached the door, he heard Hank snoring.

John entered, purposely slamming the door behind him. Hank sat up straight, squinted his eyes, yawned, and scratched his head. "Hi yea, John."

"Hi, Hank. You awake yet?" John kidded.

"Yeah, yeah," he replied, sitting on the edge of the bed. "What time is it?"

"Three o'clock. How did it go with you and that Raymond guy?"

"Okay." Hank handed him the lease and the receipt for the first month's rent.

They rested until six, and then they left for Ben's.

*   *   *

Kay was standing behind the counter when they walked in. She watched them intensely as they filed past her to join Marty and Hal, who were in the far corner. Once seated, John looked around the diner and thought, *How the hell does this guy stay in business?* In the near-empty place, he counted seven customers, including the four in his group. Other than them, he saw only a man and woman preoccupied with their meals and one man dining alone.

Out of the corner of his eye, John caught sight of Kay walking directly toward his side of the table.

"Hi. What'll ya have tonight?" she asked as she stared at John, a twinkle in her large brown eyes.

John ordered roast beef with mashed potatoes and beer. The others ordered the same.

"Bottle or draft?" she asked with a sensual voice, her lips turned up at the corners.

"Bottle would be okay, thanks," John answered politely.

She turned and strutted away with a deliberate wiggle, confident that John would be watching her every move. But it was Marty who watched her. "Man. I can feel my heart pulsating," Marty said. "She's awesome, John, and she's coming on to you. You'll have her creaming in her pants." Marty beamed.

John was pissed at Marty's remark but let it slide this time. He had more important things on his mind—like the heist.

Kay emerged from the kitchen, balancing a full tray on her left shoulder. She headed toward the four thieves' table. Her eyes were focused on John the entire way. She carefully placed her tray on a nearby stand, bending over to allow the guys a better view of her voluptuous anatomy. Juggling for table space, she speedily served them their meals.

While they were eating, John brought Marty and Hal up to date. "We rented a building located on North and Ridgeway. It's the perfect location for a control point. In fact, we'll have our first meeting there in the morning, eliminating meetings here. Marty, you and Hal meet me outside my rooming house at eight. From there you can follow me to the shop."

Kay returned to clear the table. "Care for coffee, tea, or dessert?" She again directed her question to John.

"No, thanks. That will be all," John said before requesting the check.

She appeared disappointed because John paid little or no attention to her. She fumbled with the checkbook and dropped it. Embarrassed, she picked it up and placed their check on the table. John paid the tab and they left.

CHAPTER 3

After stopping for coffee on the way, the guys arrived at the building at 8:50. Marty parked the car and dropped the tools at the far corner of the building.

Hal and Marty were impressed as they inspected the building. Afterward they all gathered in the office to discuss John's plan. John flopped into the only chair while the guys stood.

"Before I explain plan B, I want to check out the bank a few more times, specifically the alarm system."

The guys stared at John, confused, and then looked at each other. Yet they dared not question him.

"Okay, Marty, let's go and see just how tough that bank is to crack," John said. On the way, they stopped by their rooming houses to change their clothes. John put on a dark gray worsted business suit. Marty wore a white shirt, black slacks, a red silk tie, and a black leather jacket.

They walked into the bank a little after ten. There were tellers on the right, behind bulletproof glass and under a huge mural on the wall that welcomed customers to the Worthington Citizens Bank. To the left was a table where color-coded slips of pink and blue papers were neatly stored. There were large un-obscured windows along the other wall. John and Marty were approached and greeted by a guard in a loose-fitting tan uniform. "Can I help you, gentlemen?" he asked with a courteous smile.

As usual, John did the talking. "Yes, thank you. I want to inquire about renting a safe deposit box and possibly opening an account."

"Fine," the guard said, directing John to a young blonde sitting behind a desk wearing a conservative navy blue suit. Her hair was teased high, stiff with spray. The nameplate on her desk read, "Anna Marie Brooks."

Miss Brooks stood up and greeted John. "Good morning. How can I help you?" she asked politely.

"Yes, thank you. My name is Mr. London, and this is my associate, Mr. Lee. We want to rent a safe deposit box."

Miss Brooks smiled and told John that a box rental cost forty dollars per month. John immediately agreed to the price. Miss Brooks thanked him and gave him an application form, which John completed with false information.

Once the paperwork was finished, Miss Brooks escorted them to the box location. They entered a side room lined with tiny drawers. Using her master key, she unlocked the drawer and took out the safe deposit box that was two inches high, six inches wide, and eighteen inches deep. "I can carry your deposit box to the privacy booth, sir," she said, motioning to a small room off to one side containing a small table and a chair.

"No, thank you, I won't need it today." John smiled.

Miss Brooks then explained the signing procedure to be used to gain access to their box. "Any teller may assist you with your deposit box," she said, giving John a key. "This is your key, which you must present to the teller every time you need access to your deposit box." John nodded.

She secured the deposit box and led them back to her desk. "Are there any other questions?" she asked. John thought for a second, then asked about the bank's security, convincing her that he intended to deposit a large amount of money. She said, "No problem, Mr. London. I understand your concern. This bank is very secure with an excellent safety record. No one in his or her right mind would attempt to break into this building. There have been two unsuccessful hold-up attempts." She proudly explained the bank's policies and security procedures.

The bank was airtight all right, with only two doors in the entire bank, one revolving door at the front entrance and a rear emergency door. A sign posted on the door read, "Alarm will sound when the door opens." *Strange*, John thought. Most bank buildings had at least three entrances. This one, however, was a fortress.

John opted against inquiring about the alarm system at this time. "Thank you for your time, Miss Brooks. I'll return in a day or so to discuss opening an account."

*　　*　　*

Hal was anxiously awaiting John's return. John walked to the office and immediately turned to Hal and said, "Like all banks, it appears tough, but it's not tough enough to discourage me. I'm positive that plan B is solid."

Hank, not really paying attention said, "Do you think we should give on it, John?"

John flew into a rage. "Don't ever mention quitting to me again," he screamed, banging his fist against the wall. "As I said before, I'll decide what method to use to take that bank." Suddenly, one could hear a pin drop.

"Close shop," John said regaining his composure. "We'll chow down at Ben's tonight." John decided maybe a little relaxation would be good for them.

*　　*　　*

Kay's eyes lit up when John and the guys entered Ben's Diner. She quickly followed close behind them as they went to their table. They ordered beers. When Kay returned with the beers, she looked directly at John and asked, "What will it be tonight?"

Marty, not heeding John's previous warning, turned to Kay and said, "I'll have the beef 'n beer and you, honey."

"Who said anything about helping you buster?" she retorted, which embarrassed Marty.

John leveled an evil stare at Marty and ordered the veal platter. Hal and Hank ordered the beef and beer. Taking their order, Kay cat-walked back to the kitchen.

John turned to Marty and said, "What must I do to make you understand? By acting like a horny punk, you could jeopardize the success of the heist."

"Okay. Okay. I hear ya. It won't happen again."

Returning with their orders, Kay purposely served John last. In doing so, she intentionally tipped the beer glass just enough to allow the cold brew to spill over onto his lap and down his pant leg. He stood up and angrily brushed his trousers with his napkin.

"Oh, I'm so sorry," she said, peering into his eyes. She led him to a small room behind the kitchen where she kept her personal belongings. She took a hair dryer in hand and with slow deliberate strokes, she directed the hot air to the wet spot of his trousers. When she got to his crotch, John grasped her hand, "Look!"

"Kay's the name, handsome." She gave John a tantalizing, suggestive stare. The more she talked the better the offer sounded.

John had the power to abstain when he had to. And now was one of those times when he had to resist. Responding to Kay's seduction could screw up the heist operation. His plans and this relationship would not mix. "Look. We've been here too long. Your boss is looking this way, and my friends are hungry. Maybe some other time." He pushed by her and returned to his table.

When he returned to the table, John immediately told the guys, "Not one remark from anyone." Instead of relaxation, all that John got from the night was more aggravation. John told Marty to be at the shop at nine in the morning and they left.

*　　*　　*

Hal and Marty were already at the shop when John arrived. He sat at the desk, looked at the three of them, and said, "Since we have this building for thirty days we might as well use the time to set up a front by going into the auto repair business."

Marty interrupted, "You mean an actual shop, John?"

"You got it. Since you're the mechanical whiz, you'll be in charge. We must appear as professional as possible. For starters, we'll need a sign posted at the front of the building." With a twist of his wrist, he pointed his finger at Hal.

"That's you Hal. Just make a token sign, say two by two feet. Call it Marty's Auto Repair Center. I want the sign done and posted on the garage door not later than tomorrow. Got that?"

"No sweat."

John gave him money to purchase the necessary materials. Hal took the keys to the station wagon and left in search of a lumberyard.

"Marty, you and Hank take my car and see if you can find a cheap pickup truck." John gave Marty money. "Any junker will do. We'll clean it up and paint the name and address on the doors. As I said earlier, it will help us move about town without drawing suspicion. Besides, it will give us a chance to see how the law operates. Purchase the truck as far from town as possible, the further the better. Oh, one more thing, purchase whatever tools and equipment you will need to set up a shop." Marty and Hank left.

*   *   *

John spent most of the morning in the office studying the city map checking the bank's location and noting the main roads out of town. Later, Hal returned with the supplies he needed for the sign and immediately started working.

A thunderous noise greeted John's ears. "What the hell is that?" he asked, hurrying toward the front entrance, where he saw Marty and Hank in an old pickup. "Marty, shut that damn thing down!" John yelled. "I asked for a junker, not a wreck." John ordered the battered, old, green and white pickup pushed into the shop.

"It's okay. With a muffler and a tune-up it will be as good as new." Marty gave John his change.

"Well, at least it was cheap," he conceded. "Meanwhile, you guys get to work. I'm going to the bank and have another look around. Maybe just maybe I may able to decipher the alarm system."

Arriving at the bank, John went directly to the form counter and pretended to fill out a slip. As he did so his eyes focused on the location of the bank manager's desk and the distance between it and the bank entrance. He jotted down an estimated distance on the slip. He went to a bank teller to gain entrance to his vault box. His eyes were scanning anything that indicated an alarm system. Coming up empty, he thought that he was there too long, so he returned the box and left.

On his way back to the shop, he drove by a supermarket and saw empty wooden orange crates strewn by the sidewalk. John laughed and thought the crates would make excellent chairs for the guys, so he stopped and picked up three crates and continued to the shop.

When he returned to the shop, John found Hal diligently working on the sign. A short distance away, Marty had replaced the muffler and was completing the tune-up on the truck. Marty started the engine and the rusted, rundown truck was purring like a kitten. John was surprised. He hadn't realized that Marty was that good of a mechanic. Afterward, they gathered in the office, anxious to hear what John had to say. John told Hal to get the three crates from the car and bring them to the office.

Marty and Hank shook their heads and grinned when they saw that their chairs were orange crates. John took the chair. "Breaking through the roof is out, and plan B is in. I'll discuss plan B tomorrow." All three didn't know what to think; they could only hope that John's plan B had merit. "You guys can leave. I'm sticking around for a while. Be here in the morning by nine." John appeared exhausted.

*   *   *

With everyone else gone, all was quiet. John was ready to work on a plan B that would enable them to rob the Worthington bank, outsmart the cops, and get through the roadblocks. Most importantly, they needed to be able to defeat the alarm system. Rummaging through the desk drawers, he found a used writing pad and a stubby pencil. He looked over the city map, stared at the ceiling, and then looked at the city map again before staring at the ceiling one last time. In deep thought, tapping his forehead with the eraser end of the pencil, he began doodling. He paused, thought a while, and began doodling again, coming up empty time and time again. He'd finish a page, crush it in his hand, and toss it to the floor. This went on for quite sometime. By now the floor was littered with crushed paper. John stopped only for a cigarette now and then. With his fifth cigarette in his hand and staring into space, John thought to himself. *With all the easy banks in the world, I had to fuck with one as tough as the Worthington just to prove a point.*

But it was too late to cancel now, especially because it would mean having to face his peers after bragging about what a great bank robber he was and about how easy it was to rob the Worthington bank. John got back to work. Finally, at two in the morning, he put the pencil down, yawned, and laid his head on the desk to rest his eyes. But he fell asleep.

*   *   *

The garage door opening awakened John. He checked his watch. It was nine and the others were reporting in. He quickly picked up the crumbled papers from the floor and tossed them in the desk drawer. The others were surprised when they entered the office to find John sitting at the desk. He greeted them and explained that what had begun as a short nap had ended as a full night's sleep.

"Okay, we're now open for business. Marty, you and Hal are in charge. I'm going home to freshen up. When I return, we'll go over Plan B."

John gone, they settled in the office. They did not know what to make of the boss's action. After gathering their thoughts they came up empty. They decided to play cards to pass the time.

*   *   *

John worked feverishly to complete Plan B. He finally completed it at twelve-thirty. Arriving at the shop at twelve-fifty, he found the guys hard at work playing cards. John waited for the final hand to be played at which time he told them, "I'm hungry. We'll have lunch first, and then I'll explain Plan B."

He gave Hank money and told him to find a sandwich shop and pick up sandwiches and a six-pack. Hank was back in twenty minutes with the sandwiches and beer. They ate quickly because they were anxious to hear John's plan for the heist.

Thrilled, cocky, and confident that he had come up with a great plan, John savored their anxiety as he took his sweet time with his lunch.

*   *   *

"Plan B is a basic holdup using handguns." John mentioning guns drew concerned expressions from the others, who were no doubt remembering the last attempted robbery, during which the thieves were gunned down.

John read their expressions and said, "You guys worry too much. To put your mind at ease, there will not be a shoot-out. I promise."

The guys were relieved and smiled at each other. John continued, "The cops use Ford Tauruses in their fleet, so after the heist we'll use a police car mock-up to make our getaway through the road block and . . ."

Marty interrupted John and asked, "Where in the hell are you getting a police car?"

John turned to Marty and said, "If you give me a chance, I'll explain." John wanted to continue with the plan but decided to pause to answer Marty's question anyway. "Okay, Marty. I rented the Pontiac I'm now driving in Chicago. The same rental company has an office at the airport. I'll return the Pontiac and exchange it for a Ford. We make a replica of the police car . . . ." Again John noticed Marty staring questioningly. "There you go, Marty, being negative again. If you were the police standing at a road block, would you stop a police car speeding in your direction with lights flashing and siren blasting?"

Marty was satisfied with John's rationale.

John turned to Hal and said, "That's you, Hal. Since you're the artist, you will convert the Ford into a police car from bumper to bumper."

"No sweat, John. When I get through with that car, you won't know the difference."

"That's cool, Hal, but most importantly, somehow, someway, you must attract a policeman to bring his police car to the shop so that you can take photos that you'll need to copy. Offer him, say, a free wash and wax job. Got it?"

"Got it." Hal answered. "Okay, Marty, are you satisfied?"

Marty laughed. "You're sounding a lot better, John."

John continued, "I'm having a problem figuring out the alarm system, but I'm certain that it's not the same type of alarm used for the vault. I'll keep on visiting the bank to see if I can decipher the alarm system. That's it, phase 1 and 2 of plan B for now. I'll explain the balance of plan B in stages as we go along," John said with confidence. "One more item, Hal and Marty are the only ones to make any contact or talk with the police either in town or in the shop. Hank will only be included if necessary."

Marty again had a question. "What is the target day for the heist?"

"According to the information I received, the bank vault is loaded with money deposited by the local factories every Wednesday afternoon. If all goes according to plan, and without any glitches, we'll go three or four weeks from Thursday. However, I'm not sure of the exact time of the heist. That will be decided at a later date."

*   *   *

Eight-thirty the next morning, John and Hank arrived at the shop. Marty was with a customer. John asked Marty what was happening.

"No problem, John. A carburetor adjustment, I'll have it finished in no time." Marty was right on the money. He finished the job in exactly fifteen minutes. He used a plain piece of paper for the invoice, explaining to the customer that the printer had not yet delivered their billing pads. Marty charged twenty dollars. The customer paid him and left.

John observed the transaction between Marty and the customer. He smiled and walked into the office where Hank was dozing. He was about to shake Hank from his snooze when he saw a police sergeant entering the shop. He put his hand over Hank's mouth and pulled him to the far corner of the office. With rag in hand, Marty greeted the officer.

"Good morning, Officer. I'm Marty, the owner. That's Hal, my partner."

"Good morning, I'm Sergeant Winslow. This is my district. I saw your sign and decided to stop in and introduce myself and welcome you to the area." His eyes spanned the shop. Suddenly, he focused on the tools that were to be used for the break-in scattered on the floor. He walked toward them, knelt, and placed his hand on the jackhammer. He turned to Marty and asked, "You use jackhammers and large drills to work on automobiles?"

"No, sir." Marty answered. "They're rented for renovating the shop."

The Sergeant paused for what seemed to be forever and a day. He looked around the shop again. "Why would you want to renovate? It looks like the shop is all ready."

"Think of a good response, Marty," John said to himself, biting his lip.

Marty turned to the officer and replied, "The one lift is not enough." He walked to the area where the lift was located. "We want to build a lube pit, the type you climb into and work on a car from below."

Marty's explanation seemed to pacify the cop for the moment. He stared at Marty for a second. "Are you from the area?"

Before Marty could answer, the police car radio called for Sergeant Winslow. He rushed to the car and answered the call, waved to Marty, and sped off.

John was relieved that nothing had come of the incident. He emerged from the office and told Marty, "You did a fine job, Marty." Marty didn't answer; he was as pale as the gray rag he was holding. He wiped his brow. "I need to go to the bathroom. I think that I shit myself," Marty stuttered.

"That was close," John said. He told Hal, "Ditch the fuckin' tools now." Marty returned from the bathroom. John, realizing that Marty was still upset, decided to take him to the bank now to check out the alarm system, thinking it would allow him to regain his composure.

Before they left, John told Hal, "Find a piece of chalk and draw lines in the area where Marty showed the location of the proposed pit, in case that damn cop comes back."

Hal's face lit up as he said, "Good thinking, John. I'll start right away."

*   *   *

On the way to the bank, John stopped for coffee. He needed caffeine and was positive that Marty needed the same. John was happy to see that the waitress was young and pretty. She should bring Marty out of his shell. He ordered coffee, toast, and orange juice for the two of them. As John surmised, Marty's gaze was focused on the waitress.

Marty broke the silence. "Boy, that was a close call, John."

"You bet your ass. You did one hell of a job." John tried boosting Marty's ego. Between the "atta boy" and the pretty waitress, it seemed to work. John noticed the coloring returning to his face. John paid the check, and they drove on to the bank.

When they entered the bank, there was only one teller available. His nametag read "Mr. Jackson." He was a person who never seemed to smile or greet customers. John signed in and gave Jackson his key to the deposit box. Jackson led them to the deposit box location. Using the two keys, Jackson took the box from the enclosure and handed it to John. They entered the privacy booth. Marty asked John, "With all the female tellers, how come you always get the male tellers?"

"You mean Mr. Personality? He always seems to be the only teller not busy when I come here." They laughed. John closed the curtain just far enough to allow them to look around. "I can't tell much from here. Can you tell anything about an alarm system, Marty?" John asked.

"Not a thing. Sorry."

With no help from Marty, he completed his survey and said, "I can see conduit on the wall behind the teller's location leading from the floor to the ceiling. That could be a connection to an alarm system. However, it's difficult to tell from this location. I need to view it from a better vantage point." As John returned the box to Jackson, he looked and found Miss Brooks, who happened to be with other customers. The guard noticed John looking in Miss Brooks's direction. He informed John that Miss Brooks was busy with one customer and had one customer waiting. "Please be seated, gentlemen. She shouldn't be much longer."

John and Marty sat and waited. The delay worked out perfectly for John. It gave him more time to view the entire structure. John still couldn't detect anything about the alarm type. After waiting ten additional minutes, Miss Brooks was still busy. John felt that he had seen enough and decided to leave. John informed the guard that he would return later in the afternoon.

Driving to the shop, John turned to Marty and said, "I have no idea what type of alarm system the bank is using. I have to figure something out and quick."

When John entered the shop, Hank knew that something was wrong. He could read John like a book. "How did things go at the bank?"

"I couldn't decipher the alarm system, that's what." John sat down in a state of frustration.

Hank tried to buoy John's confidence, saying, "Aw, you'll figure it out."

"Sure, sez you." John happened to be looking around when he noticed a strange car in the shop. "What the hell is that?"

"It needs a complete brake job, and the customer will pick it up later today."

"Okay, I need some time to think, so let's keep it going." John told Hal to get a list of parts that Marty needed and pick them up. "Then you can look around for a policeman and a police car. Meanwhile, take a break." He gave Hank money to purchase a six-pack or two. He retired to the office for some serious thinking. Marty looked into the office and found John stretched out with his feet on the desk. He was leaning back on the chair with his hands cupped behind his head as he stared at the ceiling. Meanwhile, Hank returned with the beer. He was heading toward the office to offer John a beer when Marty intercepted him. "I don't think John wants to be disturbed. He looks like his mind is in orbit."

*   *   *

The three of them were playing cards and drinking beer when they heard John shout, "Sid Green, Yes! Sid Green!"

John charged from the office. "Sid Green's our answer. He knows every alarm system that exists." John was exuberant.

The boys were surprised and thought that John had lost his mind, but Hank knew of Sid. He and Hank had shared the same cell in prison.

Many knew Sid Green's reputation as an expert safe cracker. He had spent twenty of his fifty-two years in the Joilet state penitentiary. Sid had been John's idol growing up. They lived in the same neighborhood. Although Sid accumulated big bucks while performing his trade, the horses and compulsive gambling took the bulk of his hoard. Now, to survive and to support his horse betting, Sid worked at Abe's Deli on the east side of Chicago, eight hours a day, six days a week, except when he took time off to frequent the race track.

John asked Hank, "What's the name of the place where Sid spends most of his time on the east side?"

Hank thought awhile, then said, "Abe's. Yes, Abe's Deli, John!"

"Address, Hank. Can you remember the address?"

"Sure, Second and Webster Street."

"Cool." John only had a dollar-fifty in change so he solicited change from the guys totaling five dollars and fifty cents. John was off to find a coin phone. With help from the operator, John dialed the deli's phone number.

"Sid who?" said the voice on the other end of the line. "Sid Green, Green." John yelled.

"Oh, Sid Green. Sorry, you just missed him." He left for the track. Who's calling?"

"John Reed, a friend. When do you expect him back?" John asked.

"He should be back around six thirty."

"Fine. Tell him that I called and will call back at seven o'clock tonight. It's very important that I talk to him."

"Okay, I'll let him know as soon as he gets back."

John returned to the shop and explained his appointment to talk with Sid that night. For the first time that day, John felt confident. He knew that Sid could decipher the alarm system. He released everyone for the remainder of the day and settled in the office to relax until seven, when he could call Sid.

He propped his feet on the desk. While relaxing, all he could think about were the various types of alarm systems the bank could be using, but he kept coming up empty. Finally, fatigue set in and he dozed off. He awoke precisely at seven. He secured the shop and went and used the same coin phone as before. When the phone was answered, he asked for Sid.

"Sure. Hold on," said a raspy voice.

Sid answered the phone, his mouth full of food.

"Yeah, this is Sid. Who's this?"

"John Reed," John answered.

"Hey John! How are you doing? When did you get out?" Sid seemed overly excited to hear from John.

"Three months ago. How are you hitting them at the track these days?"

"Terrible, John. I couldn't beat those fucking nags if the races were fixed, but I keep playing the bastards! What can I do for you?"

"Well, Sid, there's this bank that I'm interested in, and I don't know the type of alarm system it's using. So I'll need your expertise to tell me determine the type of alarm and how tough it is to . . . ."

"No problem, John, I'd be happy to help."

"You're not afraid to fly, are you?"

"Hell, no. You could throw a seven anywhere, anytime. Besides, I'm too old to worry which way I kick off."

"Good," John retorted; he then informed Sid of the daily flights between Chicago and Ohio that were available to him. John emphasized that the flight time took between one and two hours.

"No problem. Give me the phone number there, and I'll check with the airlines for the earliest flight out of O'Hare tomorrow. Call you back in five or ten minutes."

"Hold on a second, I'm having a problem making out the number." John finally pieced the number together and gave it to Sid. He hung up the phone and waited for Sid to call back. As luck would have it, a kid decided to use the phone. To make matters worse, he appeared to be calling his girlfriend. After ten minutes, John asked the kid if he were going to be much longer. The kid ignored him and continued talking. John waited five additional minutes and then offered the kid ten bucks, but the boy continued giving John the cold shoulder. John finally ran out of patience, snatched the phone from the kid's hand, and hung it up. The kid turned on John, but before he could say or do anything, he was transfixed by John's vacant sub-zero stare.

The kid paused a second, called John a prick, and ran off. As he turned toward the telephone, John smiled. He savored a quick replay of intimidating the kid. *Why shouldn't I feel good?* John thought. *I'm doing business and all he wants to do is get laid.* The phone rang. John immediately answered it.

"Hey, who was on the damn phone?" Sid asked.

"Sorry, Sid. It was some kid talking to a girl. I finally had to boot him in the ass." John laughed.

"All set. I have a nine-thirty flight tomorrow morning." Sid filled him in on the airline and flight number.

"Do you want me to wire you money for the flight?"

"No problem. If I run short, I'll hit Abe for a loan."

"Great! I'll pick you up at the airport at eleven o'clock. Thanks again. I sure appreciate what you're doing for me."

"Anything for an old friend. See ya tomorrow."

On the way back to his rooming house, John realized that he hadn't had dinner, so he stopped at a deli and picked up a sandwich, coffee, and a newspaper. He ate his sandwich while he read the newspaper. Afterwards he turned on the radio and took a shower. While he was showering, Hank had returned and immediately changed the station to country music. When John stuck his head out from the shower and heard different music, he knew Hank was back. "If you keep messing with my music, Hank, I'm going to wrap that radio around your neck."

Hank changed the station back to its original music and stuck his head in the bathroom as John was toweling himself dry.

"How did things go with Sid?"

"Fine."

John explained that Sid was going to evaluate and solve the alarm system. "If anyone knows alarms, Sid's the man. In any case, I'll know what I'll be dealing with."

"That's great," Hank said before retiring for the evening. John finished reading the paper while he sipped a glass of wine. Then he turned in for the night.

At eight the next morning, everyone was settled in the office drinking coffee. John turned to them and said, "Okay. Listen up. I'll pick up Sid at the airport at eleven and take him directly to the bank. Afterwards I'll drive him back to the airport." John then turned to Hal and reminded him, "Don't forget your mission in town to look for a policeman."

Hal gave John the thumbs up and left.

At nine o'clock, John prepared to leave for the airport. He told Marty, "I probably won't be back until late in the afternoon, so you and Hank hold down the fort. One more thing: keep your eyes open for that nosy sergeant."

CHAPTER 4

Meanwhile, in the center of town, Hal was about to enter the parts store when he noticed a police car parked a short distance away. A policeman was checking parking meters. Instead of entering the store, Hal walked to the truck and began looking around as if lost. The policeman noticed Hal and approached him, asking, "Something wrong?"

"No, nothing, officer," Hal answered. "Somebody called the shop for service. I think that it was a false alarm." Hal pointed to the sign on the truck. "I work for Marty's Auto Repair. I guess somebody was being wise."

The officer sympathized with Hal. "The police and fire department also get calls that are false alarms. Marty's, eh?" The policeman glanced at the sign on the truck.

Hal sensed that he had the perfect policeman for his project. "Yes, we opened the shop this week."

"I see," said the officer. "That's the same location that Al Bonski had his shop a year ago. Business was so bad that he lost everything he invested and almost lost his wife over the ordeal." The officer continued, "The reason the shop failed is, there's not that much traffic in that area."

Hal smiled. "Were giving it a shot anyway, and I hope that it pans out better than it did for the other guy."

"Well I sure hope so, for your sake."

"Sure. Thanks a lot." Turning to the police car, Hal asked the officer if he were responsible for keeping his vehicle clean.

"Yes, we are. We get inspected at the end of each patrol. I use the local car wash, and they do a piss poor job at that."

"I know what you mean. Tell you what. If you could leave your car at the shop a few hours one day, I'd be happy to wash and wax it for you. It would only cost you a beer."

That brought a joyful reaction from the officer. "It would surely keep me in good with the Sarge." He thought for a few seconds and then told Hal, "I could drop it off Friday morning at eight in the morning and pick it up at eleven."

"Good enough," Hal said. "I'll be looking for you Friday morning at eight. By the way, what's your first name?"

"Seth. Seth Goody," he answered. Seth Goody stood tall and thin. He had straight, dirty blonde hair and appeared to be anyone other than a police officer. He asked Hal his name.

"Paul," Hal lied. "Gotta go, Seth. See you on Friday at nine." Before the officer could say goodbye, Hal was in his truck.

*   *   *

Sid was already waiting curbside when John arrived at the airport. He had no problem spotting Sid, who was wearing a maroon sports coat and maroon and white checkered slacks. The toupee he was wearing must have been found in a five and ten cent store. The huge cigar stuffed in the corner of his mouth punctuated the whole shocking picture. Laughter spread across John's face. The two men embraced in a hearty welcome, and then they walked back to the car, and they were on their way to Worthington.

"So what's with this bank, John?" Sid asked.

"A con in prison told me about it," John lied. "Its value is at least two million in cash. It sounded good to me, so I'm looking it over with the thought of possibly knocking it off. Breaking-in is out after checking it out. It's a fortress so the other option is a stick-up, but I can't tell what kind or even if there is an alarm system. I saw conduit on the walls that means nothing to me. That's where you come in, Sid."

"No problem, John. When are you thinking about knocking off the bank?"

"Oh I don't know, Sid. It's only an idea right now. It will take a lot of planning even after I complete my study." Again, John felt that four people were ample for the job.

"Well, if you decide to go for it, John, you can count me in."

"Sure. You got it." John lied.

They arrived in Worthington about twelve thirty. John told Sid that they would have lunch first, and then look over the bank. "I forgot to ask, are you staying overnight?"

"No, John. I have a four-thirty flight back to Chicago today. I have to help Abe in the morning." John was happy to hear that.

When they arrived at the bank, John gave Sid twenty dollars and told him to exchange the paper money for quarters so that he would not look too conspicuous. "If you require more time, check out the pamphlets and applications for auto loans and credit cards. I'll wait in the car."

After sitting in the hot car a spell, John was feeling uncomfortable; it appeared that Sid was in the bank for hours. The waiting and the heat were beginning to play on his mind. He looked at his watch. *Christ. He's been in the bank twenty damn minutes already.* To John's relief, Sid finally came out.

Sid apologized for the delay. "Sorry, John. I needed more time than I figured. It's an alarm all right, and a silent type to boot. The tellers, including the manager, each have one at their feet. There's a central cut-off switch located on the wall directly behind where the tellers are located."

"I was afraid of that. What if the outside cable were to be cut?"

"No. They thought of that. If you were to cut the cable, it would go off automatically at the police station."

"That takes care of that. Any ideas?"

"I'll have to sleep on it a while. I'm sure that I can come up with something. Call me in a day or so, and I'll give you my recommendation then."

"Fine. You gave me enough to go on. I'll call you."

They arrived at the airport this time with an hour to spare. John thanked Sid and handed him five hundred dollars for the airfare and his time.

"Aw, you don't have to pay me. After all, you're a friend," said Sid.

"That's what friends are for. I really appreciate what you did for me. Besides, you need it for the ponies." They laughed. After they said their goodbyes, Sid walked into the terminal and John had another long ride home.

*　　*　　*

John arrived in Worthington after five. He drove by the shop but it was closed, so he went home. When he arrived home, Hank was nowhere to be found. He took a hot shower and a brief nap. When he awoke, Hank was still missing. For dinner, John decided to dress up, so he wore his finest suit. He selected La-Bish restaurant, the town's best. As he was escorted to his table, he turned the heads of every woman in the restaurant. He placed his order of shrimp over a bed of rice and his usual Bourbon. Two young ladies seated at the next table stared and smiled at him. It made him feel uneasy. Meal consumed, he paid the check and retreated to the bar for an after-dinner drink of Grand Marnier. Suddenly he noticed one of the ladies heading his way with big flirtatious eyes. He quickly placed a ten-dollar bill on the bar and left.

John heard Hank snoring. He quickly slipped into bed and was thankful Hank did not wake up and ask a million questions.

*　　*　　*

The next morning, John and Hank arrived at the shop to find Hal and Marty already there. John could not help noticing the sheepish grin flashing across Hal's face. "Okay, Hal. It must be good news. You inherited a million dollars."

"You bet your sweet ass, John. I found the perfect patsy for my project. A policeman by the name of Seth Goody."

John congratulated him. "Good job, Hal. When will the car be here?"

"Friday morning at eight. We'll have at least three hours to clean, wax, and copy." Hal said with a grin.

John asked Hal if three hours would give him the time he needed to wax and make a copy of the car. "No problem, John." Hal answered. "If we need additional time, I'll have him return the car for a final wax job." Hal gave John the paint number written on a piece of paper.

"I'll require a minimum of five quarts of paint, a quart of additives, and a quart of paint thinner to complete the job.

"Complete the list, Hal. I'll pick up the supplies tomorrow somewhere other than Worthington. Purchasing that type of merchandise in town may draw the attention of a local paint dealer."

Hal completed the list and handed it to John. "The list includes a paint sprayer and electric polisher," he said.

With no business, they sat around and played cards. Later, John, in a happy state of mind, decided to treat the guys to dinner in town. Driving Marty and Hal to their place to clean up, John told them he would pick them up at seven. John and Hank continued to their place to clean up and dress.

Marty and Hal were waiting curbside when John arrived. After cruising around, John found the steak house he had noticed the last time he was in town. The hostess escorted them to their table. The aroma of the steaks sizzling on the open hearth piqued their appetites. John ordered the most expensive steaks on the menu with all the trimmings for everyone, as well as a fine red wine.

Afterward, John ordered a round of after-dinner drinks. While they were sipping their drinks, Hank happened to look to his right and saw what he probably thought to be the most beautiful girl he had ever seen. He admired her with his eyes. Her companion noticed Hank staring and took offense. He dropped his napkin on the table and walked over to Hank, shouting and calling him a degenerate. It caught Hank by surprise, as he had meant no harm.

John sensed trouble and saw Hank's face turning colors, so he tried to pacify the man, explaining that Hank was merely admiring his friend and the gesture really should be taken as a compliment. The guy still carried on, would not accept John's explanation, and took a swipe at Hank. John's patience finally ran out. He landed a left hook to the man's stomach, then a smashing right hand to the chin, which sent the guy sprawling unconscious to the floor. The guy never knew what had hit him.

Meanwhile, the management had already contacted the police, who arrived at the restaurant within minutes. Hal had the smarts to realize that the police should not see them together. He motioned Hank and Marty to the men's room and out of sight.

The manager immediately fingered John as the troublemaker. The police cuffed and shoved John into the police van and took him away.

*   *   *

At the police station, the police knew that John was an out-of-towner. To make matters worse, the sergeant on duty was the meanest officer in the precinct. He was the first to speak. "We have a quiet town here. We don't like garbage like you coming here and polluting it."

"I did nothing wrong. I was just passing through and stopped for a bite to eat. I don't like being picked on by any one, especially when I'm minding my own business."

"Oh, a wise bastard," said the sergeant. He smacked John across the face, drawing blood from his lip. John did all he could to keep his cool.

"After we are through with you, you'll know that we mean to keep trash like you out of our town. Now empty your pockets and let me see your identification. John Reed from Chicago. It doesn't surprise me. Any police record John Reed?" John saw his plans crumbling before him. "Well, speak up trash man."

"No. No police record other than a speeding ticket," John lied.

"All right, Mr. Reed, you have one phone call before I throw you in the can."

John declined the phone call and was taken to the cell. He was upset, but mostly he was concerned that they would check his police record and screw up his parole, not to mention the heist. He did not sleep all night for fear that they would check his police record. In fact, he heard the changing of the shift and learned that the Sergeant's name was Nelson.

After explaining the details to Sergeant Nelson, the night sergeant left the station house. Sergeant Nelson came to John's cell. "Care to wash up, Mr. Reed?"

"Thanks. I surely could use a bathroom." The new sergeant seemed more humane.

John returned from the bathroom and was told to sit in the office.

Sergeant Nelson glanced at the complaint sheet, then glanced at John and said, "Chicago, Mr. Reed?"

"Yes sir. I was returning to Chicago and decided to get a bite to eat. The rest is what you see on the sheet. All I wanted was to have dinner and be on my way, but the guy started a fracas for no particular reason. I tried to explain to him in a nice way, but then he called me a degenerate. Unfortunately, I lost my cool."

Sergeant Nelson grinned. "The judge is not due in for another hour. He will read the charges and listen to your rebuttal and then decide your guilt or innocence. In the meantime, relax, and have a cup of coffee until then."

For the next hour John's eyes were focused on the radio. His luck was still holding out. No one attempted to check his record with the police in Chicago.

Meanwhile, the judge arrived and was given the police report. He glanced over it and looked up at John before glancing at the report again. He directed John to stand. "How to do you plead, Mr. Reed?"

"Not guilty, sir."

"Well, Mr. Reed, you did disturb the peace. That is a town ordinance and a violation. I don't see a complaint filed by the person you assaulted. I herby fine you two hundred and fifty dollars or ten days in jail."

John didn't hesitate. He reached for his wallet on the desk, handed the clerk the money, and was released.

John thanked the judge and walked briskly to the exit. Reaching the sidewalk, he took off as fast as he could. He looked for and eventually found public transportation that took him within walking distance of the shop.

*   *   *

When he arrived at the shop, he found the door locked. He knocked what seemed to be a dozen times before Hal let him in. As he entered the shop, Hank and Marty were gathered in the office. Upon seeing John, they converged on him like a swarm of bees. Arty was the first to speak, as he looked at John's battered face.

"Looks like they did a number on you, the mother-fuckers," Marty said, taking a closer look at John's bloody lip.

"Could have been worse, Marty. You find some good cops, and you find bastards. I drew the short straw on this one. I'll survive."

Hank approached John, "I'm sorry, John. I didn't mean to cause trouble."

"It wasn't your fault, Hank." John said. "You didn't do anything that any normal guy wouldn't have done under the same circumstances. The bastard tried to act like a big shot in front of his girl."

Marty asked John for the details, and John answered by saying, "I consider myself very lucky. They didn't bother to check out my police record."

"I'll say you were lucky," Marty replied.

"I'm going home to freshen up and get some shut eye," John said. "I'm really beat. You guys relax today, and we'll get back to normal operations tomorrow morning." Hank gave John the keys to the car and they watched as John walked slowly to his car to drive home.

*   *   *

John hurried up the front steps so as not to be seen by the landlady. He knew that she was standing behind the curtain. He tried his best to conceal his face. When he reached his room he disrobed immediately and jumped into the shower. Afterwards he looked in the mirror to view the damage done to his face. His lip was busted up badly, his left eye puffed. He had two days' growth of hair on his face, so he thought he'd grow a mustache that would no doubt change his looks a little. Feeling really tired, he went to bed.

John slept through the day and the night. Hank had gone home with Marty and Hal to spend the night, so as not to disturb him. He awoke before seven the next morning and felt a lot better. He went to the bathroom and looked in the mirror. He had a fat lip and resembled a prizefighter. He brushed his teeth gently and decided not to shave. It then dawned on him that Hank was not at home. He hoped that Hank had not left for causing trouble.

"Na, Hank isn't that sensitive." He laughed to himself, but the laugh was on him: it caused his lip to crack and bleed.

Before heading for the shop, John took his suitcase out from under the bed and opened it to reveal the secret compartment that held his seed money. He took inventory and then took the money needed to purchase the paint and materials. John also replenished the funds he used to pay his fine.

*   *   *

The guys were in the shop office busy doing nothing when John walked in. Marty was the first to greet him. "Hi, John, You look a lot better. How are you feeling?"

"A lot better," John answered.

Marty then asked John, "What's on the agenda for today?"

"Hank and I will drive to the shopping center and pick up the paint supplies. If time allows, I'll exchange the Pontiac for the Ford. Meanwhile, you and Hal keep a sharp lookout for that nosey sergeant."

*   *   *

John and Hank were on their way to pick up the supplies, ten miles out and still looking for the next town. "I should have asked directions or checked a map, Hank. I could have sworn that I passed a town on my way from the airport to Worthington."

"We have to hit a town sooner or later," Hank told John.

John did not comment. He just shook his head, and as he did so he noticed that Hank was growing a beard. It made Hank appear much older, but John wisely kept his opinion to himself.

As they rounded a sharp bend of the road, they happened upon a huge shopping center. "How's that for luck, Hank? Now if only there is a paint store in this complex, we've got it made." For the second time, John got lucky. You could not miss the sign JAY'S PAINT CENTER located at the middle of the shopping center complex.

The store clerk was very helpful. He explained everything that one needed to know about painting a car plus some additional tips that John jotted down in his notebook.

The clerk did not go un-rewarded: he sold John the most expensive paint sprayer and an electric polisher. John thanked him and left. On the way out, they passed a doughnut shop. Hank stopped and gazed at the display of assorted sweets. John noticed and smiled. Being in a good mood, he handed Hank five dollars, "Here, buy yourself a dozen."

After Hank purchased the doughnuts, John glanced at his watch. "Let's have lunch and then head back to the shop. I'm not up to riding to the airport today to pick up a Ford."

Hank had eaten the last of the doughnuts by the time they arrived at the shop. John noticed the leftover cream on Hank's face and beard. He looked comical. John shook his head and said, "You'd better wipe the cream from your chin before we get inside or you'll leave yourself open for Marty's nasty jokes."

* * *

Hank opened the garage as door John drove into the shop. John looked around and was happy to see no customers. Hal helped Hank unloaded the supplies and took inventory. After checking item by item against his list, Hal was satisfied. He stowed the supplies in the paint booth.

When he did not see the Ford, Marty asked, "What about the Ford?"

John frowned. "Ford? Do you see the Ford?"

"I wouldn't have asked if I'd seen one. Would I?"

"That means that I didn't pick up the Ford, and furthermore I'll pick up the Ford when I'm good and ready. Does that answer your question?" John glared at him.

"I don't give a damn if you pick it up or not."

* * *

At eight o'clock the next morning everyone assembled in the shop office. The guys were waiting to see what John had to say. John still appeared annoyed at Marty because of the previous day's questioning. John just sat with a cigarette in his hand staring at the ceiling. Taking a final extensive drag, he inhaled as he held his head back, suspending the smoke at the back of his throat. Finally he exhaled and the smoke floated toward the ceiling. He crushed the cigarette on the desk.

"Okay, listen up. I'm ready to explain phase 3 of plan B. Since today is Thursday and Thursday is the day of our planned heist, it's the perfect opportunity to check out the best hour of the morning to pull off the heist with the least amount of people around. I don't like sticking up a bank crowded with people. It can be difficult controlling a large crowd. Also, I am eliminating the first week of the month because that's when all the old bastards cash their social security checks. So the exact time of the heist will be determined by the hour averaging the least amount of people on a Thursday morning between nine and noon."

This time it was Hal who asked John a question. "How are you planning on determining the exact time?"

John turned to Hal and said, "Each of us will take turns observing the bank and keeping count of people entering and leaving. We begin this morning." John checked his watch. "I'll take the first shift at nine til nine-thirty. Hank will follow me with the nine-thirty to ten shift because I decided that Hank and I will pick up the Ford today. Marty, you'll take the ten to ten-thirty shift. Park the truck on the street in full view of the bank. Pretend to be trouble-shooting a problem with the truck and observe the bank from that vantage point. Hal, you'll follow with the ten-thirty to eleven, shift. Pretend to be filling out a deposit slip or a loan application. Ask for change, anything to buy yourself enough time. Marty, you and Hal will spend the final hour observing the bank from the restaurant located on the opposite side of the street. It's a perfect vantage point; get seated by the window."

John continued with emphasis, "I repeat, the exact time of the heist will be determined by the hour averaging the least amount of customers that are in the bank." He suddenly noticed Hal staring at him, smiling. "Hal?" John asked.

"Nothing, John. I was just noticing your moustache; it's almost fully grown! I must admit that it makes you appear rather dapper." Hal smiled.

On the other hand, Hank's beard did not fare as well. Good ol' Marty had to make a derogatory remark: "Hank, with your beard you look like Tolouse Lautrec, the French Artist." Hank had no idea who Tolouse Lautrec was, but he sensed that he should be insulted. Hal burst out laughing. However, John didn't think that it was funny.

"Aw, screw you," Hank said, finally realizing that Marty was poking fun at his beard.

Marty approached Hank with open arms, and embraced him. "Only kidding, Hank. I was just having a little fun."

John became pissed. He turned to Marty and said, "Just having little fun is going to get you in trouble one of these days." Marty just ignored John's comment.

*   *   *

It was approaching nine o'clock when John drove into the bank's parking lot. The lot was already full of cars. Walking toward the bank, John looked at the many cars. He wondered if most of them belonged to bank employees or to customers.

Entering through the revolving doors, John passed the guard and saw only two tellers on duty. They were already busy with customers and six more were waiting in line. The lines were moving slowly. After ten minutes of waiting, he was now the third person in line. Five additional people came in after him.

John backed out of the line and went to the counter containing deposit slips. He scribbled some notes on a few slips. Having stalled long enough, he scanned the bank a final time and walked deliberately toward the exit and left. John immediately ruled out nine and ten o'clock as possible time frames for the heist.

When John arrived at the shop, Hank was ready to jump in the car for his vigil. John stopped him and led him to the shop office. Hank was stuttering as they walked. Marty and Hal also appeared puzzled.

John assured them that there was no problem. "There's no need for Hank to take his nine-thirty to ten shift because of what I observed while in the bank. The large volume of customers will continue well into ten. Marty, you and Hal will take your turns as originally planned. Me and Hank are leaving for the airport. I expect to be back between two and three o'clock."

Shortly before ten o'clock, Marty left for the bank. As if by design, he found the perfect parking space from which he could view both the bank entrance and the parking lot. He raised the hood of the truck. His watch began. Six customers exited while five entered within twenty minutes. The count did not fair well with Marty and he thought about leaving.

Suddenly he heard, "Marty's Auto Repairs!" Startled, Marty looked up. In doing so, he whacked his head against the hood. Rubbing his head, he turned to see a police officer standing over him. Marty was speechless.

The officer smiled again and apologized and said, "My name is Seth. Seth Goody. I was talking to Paul the other day about my squad car . . . ."

Marty looked at him again and wondered what the hell he wanted. Suddenly, Marty realized that this was the police officer Hal had lined up for the polish job. Obviously Hal had used a phony name. Now his head was really hurting.

"Ohhh. Seth Goody. Sure, sure. You have to forgive me. It's early, and this darn truck is giving me a damned problem." As he tried hard to keep track of people entering and leaving the bank, he said, "Sure, Paul told me about you bringing your car in Friday morning." Marty excused himself, "I gotta get back to the shop."

"Sure, I understand." Seth bid his farewell and left to protect the town.

Between banging his head, the heart palpitations generated by Officer Goody, and trying to keep count of customers, Marty was just about done in. So he slammed the hood shut and returned to the shop to see if Hal would take the remainder of his shift because of his injury. He told Hal what he had observed so far; ten and ten-thirty were not good.

"No problem, Marty. Sit and rest. I'll return in about an hour or so."

Hal left for his shift.

*   *   *

John and Hank arrived at the airport at eleven o'clock. It was good timing but it took almost fifteen minutes to walk from the parking lot to the National Auto Rental.

A tall blonde greeted them. She was in her late twenties. "How can I help you?" she asked as she looked into John's eyes.

Before John could answer, Hank intervened: "Could you help us? Boy could you help us!" It seemed strange that Hank could be so outspoken without John becoming upset. But it seemed that Hank had a mystifying hold on John.

John, surprised by Hank's action, was embarrassed. "Yes, thank you. But, first, I must apologize for my friend here, who just happens to be in his second childhood."

"Oh I don't mind at all," she purred. "You get used to it after a while, especially in this type of job where you get to meet interesting people."

John explained that he was returning the Pontiac to exchange it for a Ford Thaurus.

"Ford Taurus. Let's see," she said as she checked her records. "I don't have a Ford Taurus available. Sorry."

John was upset because he had planned on calling prior to making the trip to the airport and hadn't. He was about to leave. "Hold on, a sec, let me check one more source." She excused herself and pranced down the corridor. Hank's eyes followed her every move.

"Did you see the way she looked at you, John?" Hank asked excitedly.

John took a long hard look at Hank. "You know, Hank, you have one hell of an imagination. If all the young women you said went for me really did, I'd be screwing everything that moved."

Hank didn't know how to respond to John's remark, so he did the next best thing. He clammed up. He felt saved by the attendant who returned and happily informed John that someone had just returned a Ford. "It's being cleaned as we speak."

John thanked her. She quoted John the price of two hundred dollars for the two weeks, to which he immediately agreed. At her request, John surrendered the Pontiac's contract, which he retrieved from his coat pocket and handed it to her.

"Thank you, Mr. Mitchell. May I see your driver's license, please"?

"License?" John questioned.

"Yes. I'm sorry but its company policy. I know you presented it in the Chicago office but . . ."

John took his billfold from his hip pocket. He looked at her and said, "I didn't think that I looked like a suspicious character." John grinned as he fumbled through his billfold.

She paused and then answered, "Oh that's all right, Mr. Mitchell. You do have an honest face. Will you be returning the car here or in Chicago?"

"Chicago." John was relieved.

She asked him to sign the contract and leaned over to show him where he was to sign. He also leaned over and their faces almost touched. John almost forgot himself. With Hank standing nearby he quickly regained his composure and thanked her. Looking at her nametag fixed on her uniform, he said, "Debbie. Pretty name. What time do you get off from work?"

She smiled and answered, "Six." She handed John the car keys. "It's parked in the same area where you returned the Pontiac."

John thanked her again before he and Hank were on their way to the parking lot. On the way to the "down" escalator, John turned to Hank and said, "Not a word, Hank. Not a word."

Hank looked at him. "Right, John. Not a word. However I have to say, whether you get pissed or not, that you handled yourself well in there. I didn't know you needed to show your license to rent a car. I thought we were in trouble."

"We were in trouble, Hank. My license says John Reed, not Mr. Mitchell."

"Wow!" Hank shouted, realizing, John had finessed her. They picked up the car and were on their way to Worthington.

*   *   *

Back in Worthington, Hal had no trouble with his surveillance. The bank was crowded with customers. Due to the long line, he left the bank at ten forty five. He returned to the shop and found Marty in the office, his head on the desk, using his arms for a pillow. Marty woke up when Hal walked in.

"How do you feel?"

"Shitty," Marty said. "Maybe a bowl of soup would settle my stomach."

"No sweat. Our final watch is at the restaurant anyway . . . We can watch while we eat." They got into the truck and were on their way to the restaurant.

They were fortunate that seating was available by the window facing the bank. Hal volunteered to take the seat facing the bank. This would allow Marty to eat without straining his eyes. Hal began his watch.

Twenty minutes had elapsed. To Hal's surprise, only one customer entered the bank as several were leaving.

They ordered a second cup of coffee. Hal checked his watch again. Twelve forty. The count was now zero; the last customer who had entered had left the bank. Without finishing their coffee, Hal told

Marty to pay the check, then go to the truck and wait. "I want to take a final look inside the bank."

As Marty went to the truck, Hal went to the bank. He pushed through the revolving door. Without stopping, he looked in and kept moving as the door brought him back onto the street. Hal jumped into the truck. "Empty, Marty. Empty. Not a soul except for the employees." Hal checked his watch. It was twelve forty-five. Marty started the truck and they left.

*   *   *

John and Hank made good time returning to Worthington, arriving at the shop at one-thirty that afternoon. They were greeted by Hal, who guided John to a parking place at the far corner of the shop. John went to the office and found Marty sitting at the desk, looking pale as a ghost. "What's wrong, Marty? You look like shit."

"I feel like shit," Marty answered. He explained about hitting his head on the truck.

John ordered Hank to drive Marty to his rooming house to rest for the remainder of the day. He then turned his attention to Hal and asked, "How did your watch and Marty's watch go?"

"Marty's watch stunk. On the other hand my watch you won't believe. The bank was completely free of customers between twelve thirty-five and twelve forty-five," said Hal.

John thought for a moment. "It looks like twelve forty-five it is. Thursday following the completion of the police car will be the day the heist goes down. However, there could be a problem. If I can't solve the silent alarm, the heist could be delayed."

John asked Hal if all was set for tomorrow morning with the police car.

"The car will be here at eight sharp."

"That's cool. Hank and me will be here eight-thirty so we won't be seen by the cop."

"No sweat," Hal answered. He walked around the Ford for a complete body inspection and found it to be perfect. "This car will do just fine."

John asked Hank for the car keys so he could check on Marty. He was about to leave when Hal hastened to the car and stopped him.

"What's wrong?"

"Nothing serious, I just remembered that I need a camera to take photos of the police car. Can you stop by a camera shop on you way to see Marty and rent a Polaroid camera . . . .

"You got it." John started the car and was on his way to Marty's rooming house. He went directly to his room. He did not have to knock because the door was ajar. Marty was sleeping peacefully. John placed his hand on his forehead to check his temperature. *No fever. He should be fine in the morning,* John thought.

John found the camera shop and told the sales person, "I'd like to buy an instant camera. Any model will do fine." He purchased the camera and was about to leave when the salesperson asked him about film. Confused for a second, John looked at him before realizing what the salesperson meant.

"You're correct. If I want to take a picture I need film." He was upset with himself but mostly embarrassed.

When John returned to the office, Hal and Hank were playing cards. He handed the camera to Hal. Hal stopped playing cards and inspected the camera. "How's Marty?" Hank asked.

"He seems fine. I'll make him rest all day tomorrow."

Out of the clear blue, Hank thought about the alarm system and asked John if he had solved it yet.

John got to his feet. "Fuck, Hank. I completely forgot. Thanks for reminding me. I was to call Sid a few days ago to find out his recommendation for the bank alarm."

They were about to close shop and look in on Marty when a customer entered the shop. He was an older person. He appeared to be in his seventies and shuffled his feet as he walked. John hoped that Hank could handle what turned out to be loose battery cables. Hank completed the repair in ten minutes. The old guy left happy.

"Let's get the hell out of here before another customer shows up," said John, annoyed. They secured the shop and left for Marty's place.

*   *   *

On the way John told Hal to find a pay phone so that he could call Sid. Hal spotted a pay phone at a service station. John was lucky because Sid answered the phone. John apologized for not calling sooner.

"That's okay, John. I don't have great news for you anyway."

John's body stiffened. "Okay. What do you have?"

"After racking my brains, the only solution I can come up with is to have one of your guys impersonate a utility employee minutes before the heist. Tell the bank manager that the outside cable has to be checked. In order to check the cable, the system would have to be turned off. There's a fifty-fifty chance that the manager won't question or check with the utility company or the police. That's the best idea that I can come up with, John. Sorry."

"That's okay, Sid. You gave me something to go on." John was disappointed. He relayed the information to Hal and Hank.

Hal understood, but Hank with skepticism asked John, "What if it doesn't work?"

John turned to Hank and said, "You're beginning to sound like Marty, thinking negative. You use whatever tools you have to do a job." He then turned to Hal and said, "The utility idea shouldn't affect plan B; it could make the heist a little tougher, however, so, we'll have to sit in the next day or two and discuss a way to find out how the utility company operates and how to purchase a uniform and equipment that we'll need."

"You got it, John."

The extra day's rest was beneficial, for Marty was rearing to go the next day.

CHAPTER 5

Hal arrived at the shop earlier than normal to await the arrival of Officer Goody. As he waited, he fine-tuned the camera and snapped a few sample photos. Satisfied with the results, he placed the camera on the desk and anxiously waited for Goody's arrival.

Officer Goody arrived precisely at eight. After the greetings, Goody handed Hal a paper sack containing coffee and an egg sandwich. Hal thanked him and asked if he had a return ride. "Yes, sir I do, thank you. Officer Goody then informed Hal of a slight problem. Hal froze on the spot, as he feared the worst. "Sorry, but I must have the car back at the station at ten instead of eleven."

Hal, relieved, said. "No sweat, Seth. It will be waiting for you upon your return, shiny as new. One thing. Don't spread the word around the precinct about this. Let it be our little secret, okay?"

Officer Goody assured him that no one would know. "This way the Sarge will think that I worked on the car." He winked at Hal. He thanked Hal again and reminded him that he would return at ten.

When Goody left, Hal relaxed and ate the egg sandwich and finished drinking his coffee. He washed the car and prepped it for polishing. John, Hank, and Marty arrived a little after eight-thirty.

"We only have an hour and a half to finish the job due to a change in plans by that prick officer," Hal explained to John.

"Okay, let's get to work." They changed into work clothes. John checked the electric polisher while Hank brought out the clean cloth and wax.

The assembly line began. Hank applied the wax, Marty wiped it clean, John followed with the electric polisher, and Hal finished up with a clean cloth for the final touch. The wash and wax was completed in one hour and twenty minutes.

Hal picked up the camera and took photos of the car. He covered every possible angle, and when he was finished, he spread the photos on the desk to allow them to develop and dry.

Hal immediately went to work taking the measurements of the identification numbers, lettering, and the police insignia. He told John that he could not promise perfect results.

"It wouldn't matter because we would be speeding through the road block. Any imperfections wouldn't be noticed unless we were stopped. If so we would have a problem that could end with a shoot out," John said.

That remark didn't go unnoticed by the guys. Shock shone on their faces as they stared at one another.

"I'm going to the bank to look around," John said.

He was walking toward the station wagon when a horn blast from a car driven through the shop door startled him. He had to leap to one side so as not to get hit. John was reputed to be afraid of nothing and no one. But this time he was so frightened that he just about pissed himself.

John ran to the car, prepared to lambaste the driver. Before he could raise hell, he saw the driver was none other than Kay the waitress from Ben's Diner. She looked at him and smiled. "Are you open for business?" she asked.

John shook his head with disbelief. "How did you know about the shop?" he asked her.

"I recognized him," she said, pointing to Hal, "in town last week, and I saw the sign on the door of the truck . . . ."

John made the mistake of asking her, "What can I do for you?"

Her eyes lit up like a Christmas tree. "Are you putting me on, Mr . . . Say, what is your name anyway?"

"John Reed," he answered without thinking. He quickly realized he had made a blunder. Now she was the only one person in town who knew his real name. "No, I'm not putting you on." Kay noticed that John was beginning to lose his cool. Being shrewd she immediately changed the subject.

"I'm having trouble starting my car. So I thought that I might need a tune-up or repair. I figured that you could use the business."

John then told her that she would have to leave the car until later that afternoon. She agreed and asked John to give her a lift home. He answered, "I'll have one of the mechanics drive you home."

She looked at him directly and demanded, "I want you to drive me home."

Caught by surprise, John wasn't sure how to react, so he agreed. He thought that he would drive her home first then drive to the bank.

John told Marty to check her car, pick up the parts required, and make the necessary repairs.

He opened the door and helped her out of the car. As she got out, John got a full view of her shapely legs and thighs. He got the same view when she entered the station wagon. She did have a nice set of legs, even though they were on the lean side.

She gave John directions to her home, and they were on their way. There was silence. Then she turned to John and asked, "What is your real reason for being in Worthington, Mr. Reed?"

Stunned by her question, he answered, "Business." His eyes focused on the road.

"Come now, Mr. Reed. I know for a fact that's a poor location for an auto repair shop. The last person who operated a shop at that location went bankrupt. So, in essence, if one person couldn't make it work, how could four people survive and make a decent living?"

John did not answer her. They finally arrived at her apartment. "You don't want to answer?" she asked.

John turned to her, "I don't have to answer to you or anyone. Is that clear?" John was clearly upset.

"Quite clear," she answered. She opened the door half way, turned, and invited John up to her place for a drink.

"No thanks. I have to run an errand, and be on my way."

"Fine." She said. "I will be home until three in case . . ." She gave John her apartment number and invited him in for a drink when he returned with her car. "I will not take no for an answer."

"Suppose I was to send the mechanic with your car?" John answered.

"You wouldn't dare." She grinned.

John, ignoring her, did not answer. She sashayed slowly up her apartment steps. John watched as she disappeared through the entrance door. On his way to the bank he realized that he had a potential problem on his hands. Then and there, he decided to play her little game and find out what she really thought was his reason for being in Worthington.

* * *

Meanwhile, Seth Goody was shouting, "Whoowee! Wait until the sarge takes a gander! His eyes will pop out of their sockets." Seth slapped Hal on the back and asked him if there was anything that he could do for him.

He stiffed a laugh and managed a smile. "Yes, there is something you can do for me. I would like to take your photograph, standing by your car."

"Shoot. Is that all? You got it."

Hal took his picture in every conceivable position, including standing by the car, and extra photos of his uniform so that he would have clear and concise photographs. He thanked Officer Goody as he left.

Hal, with pictures in hand, walked to the office humming all the way. He placed the pictures on the desk, leaned back in the chair and laughed out loud. "The stupid fuck Goody played right into my hands."

John returned from the bank at approximately eleven thirty in the morning. Marty was working on the waitress's car. John approached him, leaned under the hood, and asked for the verdict.

"All it needed was a tune-up. I'll have it ready in about thirty minutes."

John walked to the office and found Hal hard at work on the schematic of the Ford Taurus using chart paper to size the letters and insignia. John was impressed as he watched Hal do his thing.

Marty walked into the office with rag in hand, wiping his hands clean. He informed John the tune-up was completed.

"Cool, Marty. Thanks." Being thirsty, John gave Hank money and told him to pick up a six-pack.

Hal pushed himself away from the desk, stretched his arms toward the ceiling, and said, "I surely could use a beer right about now."

They finished drinking their beer. John thought that he'd better return the car to the waitress. He took a final drag on his cigarette and tossed it to the floor.

As usual, Hank had to make a remark, "Some guys have all the luck."

"Somebody has to do it," John answered, teasing. He was on his way.

Arriving at Kay's apartment, John knocked on the door. Kay answered standing at the open door wearing a black nightgown, with a split at the sides exposing her legs up to her thigh. Wearing high heel shoes completed the awesome picture she displayed. John was shocked but impressed.

She greeted John and led him to the living room where she had him sit on a comfortable high-back chair, the kind one would find in front of a fireplace. John thanked her and paused because he had forgotten her name.

"You forgot my name? Its Kay, sweetie." She then offered John a drink.

"Yeah. Thanks. Bourbon, please." She placed a tray of hors d'oeuvres on the coffee table and sat directly opposite John, her nightgown spread open, again exposing her thighs. For a few seconds, John appeared mesmerized.

She read John's eyes and knew he was intrigued. She gave him a chance to take a sip of his drink before breaking the silence. "How do you like our town?"

"It's okay. The people are okay too." He smiled.

"How long to you plan on staying in Worthington?"

"It depends on how my business works out."

"Come on, Mr. Reed. How can four people make a decent living operating a business in that remote area of town?"

John leaned forward, picked up a miniature hot dog, and placed it in his mouth. He chewed as he stared at Kay for a few seconds, took a sip from his drink, and looked her up and down.

"Well, I'll tell you. Actually, I'm here to rob the Worthington Citizen Bank." Again, John looked her up and down and back to her thighs.

This time Kay was the one who appeared mesmerized. Suddenly she broke out in laughter. "You're putting me on, Mr. Reed. No one in their right mind would be crazy enough to try it, if they valued their lives. But I think that you are up to something besides auto repair."

John felt immediate relief. He asked her why she was concerned about his business.

She answered, "Just curious, I guess." She shifted her position to expose more of her body. John said, "You know what curiosity did to the cat?"

"You don't seem the type," she answered. She then invited him to sit next to her. She looked into his eyes and abruptly told him that she wanted his body.

John was not surprised. He paused for a few seconds and then told her that if he were to agree he didn't want a commitment. "This would be the first and last time. You are not to bother me or my friends ever again from now on, understood?"

She immediately agreed. She stood up, took John by the hand, and led him to her bedroom, where she fell back on the bed taking off her underpants. At the same time John began undressing. She lay in a prone and ready position, awed by John's masculine anatomy. By now, John was at the point of no return and began his drive. They went at it for what seemed to be a long time and ended with a grand climax together. John dressed, finished his drink, and waited as she showered and dressed for work. She drove him back to the shop.

John requested to be dropped off a block from the shop. When they arrived, Kay parked the car. She opened her purse and asked John, "How much do I owe you for the repairs?" He reached for the door handle, turned, looked at her and said that the repair was on him.

"Thank you," she said. "Hope we can get together again . . . ." John turned and reminded her of the agreement they had made just an hour ago. It was to be a first and last time. He got out of the car, thanked her for the ride, and walked to the shop.

John found Hal, Marty, and Hank sitting in the office. Hal was hard at work on the schematic. John told them, "Take a break." He took the orange crate and set it by the desk and sat.

Hank was the first to speak. "Well? Well?" John looked at him.

"Well, what Hank?"

"Anything interesting happen between you and the broad?" Even Hal and Marty leaned forward with breathless anticipation.

John was quiet. It seemed a long time before he answered. "Nothing happened, Hank. I delivered the car to her. She made me a cup of coffee. Nothing more."

The guys stared at John with a combination of surprise, envy, and, disappointment.

To change the subject and to get their minds off Kay, he asked Hal, "When will the Ford Taurus be ready to begin painting?"

"Ready to go. I'll probably work over the weekend. If all goes well, the car should be completed as scheduled."

John insisted that all of them work the weekend.

CHAPTER 6

Saturday morning the guys arrived at the garage at eight so that they could get an early start on the Ford. It was going to be a long, dirty, dusty day. John had designated Hal to be the person-in-charge of the paint project.

For the next two hours he would have them jumping through hoops. John, not used to hard labor, called for a breakfast break and wisely volunteered to pick up the food. Hank was stunned when he heard John volunteer. It was not like John to run errands. But Hal being a little wiser, knew why John had called for a break and why he wanted to make the pick-up.

The three of them were sanding the car when John returned thirty minutes later with bags of food. The aroma of bacon and fresh-brewed coffee permeated the garage. They sat and ate their breakfasts slowly, enjoying every morsel and knowing how much they needed this break. They had been working on the Ford nonstop.

Hal broke the silence, "Okay, lard asses, time's up. Back to the grindstone."

"You're a slave driver, Hal," Hank mumbled.

"We have a deadline to meet if we want to get the job done on time. We have to keep the momentum going," Hal told Hank.

They even worked through lunch. There was sanding, sanding, and more sanding. Even though they were wearing masks and safety glasses, the dust was making it difficult for them to breathe. It was Hal who called for a break this time. They washed the dirt and dust from their faces and went outside where the air was cool and fresh.

Still tired, John ordered them to the office for a break, where he sat and put his feet on the desk. He took out his Marlboro's, stuffed a cigarette in his mouth, and lit up.

They were relaxing when suddenly the police uniforms crossed John's mind. He turned to Hal and said, "Okay, Hal, now we're ready for Phase Three of plan B: police uniforms. To appear authentic driving a police car through a roadblock, Hank and I will have to wear uniforms. We'll need two shirts, two hats, and coats and ties. Perhaps you can borrow a uniform from Officer Goody. Tell him that you and a friend are going to a masquerade party and you plan on attending the party dressed as a policeman. We can use his uniform as a sample to make a duplicate."

Hal said, "What if I get a negative response from Goody?"

"Then I'll have to come up with another plan." The day ended when John looked at his watch, "It's four-fifteen. Clean up and let's get the hell out of here." John appeared exhausted.

*   *   *

John was the first in the bathroom and into the bathtub. The hot bath was therapeutically soothing to his aching muscles. The bathroom was enveloped with steam created by the very hot water. The vapors were creating a Sauna-like environment, and he could feel his body relaxing and his sinuses releasing dust particles.

Hank yelled in the bathroom, "Did you pass out in there?"

"Funny, Hank very funny. I'll be through in a few minutes," John answered. However, a few minutes turned into many minutes. He still needed to cool off in the shower and wash his hair.

Now Hank was really bitching, "Christ, John you're worse than a broad."

"Funny again, Hank."

Hank was just the opposite. He completed his shower in no time, which drew a comment from John: "Man, you finished so fast I bet you forgot to clean your private parts."

Hank ignored his remarks.

John prepared for bed, turned on the radio, and relaxed.

Hank told John, "Hal, Marty, and me are having breakfast or a brunch in the morning and maybe catch a movie. Care to come along?"

"No, Hank. I'll be sleeping late tomorrow. You guys go ahead and relax for the day." John turned over and went to sleep.

Sunday morning, Hal picked up Hank. They stopped at the Sunset Diner for a brunch that lasted through one o'clock. Afterwards they decided to catch a movie in town.

*   *   *

John awoke, sat on the edge of the bed, stretched his arms, and tried to work out the kinks in his shoulder. He put his face close to the bathroom mirror. Running his hand across his chin, he found a hairy growth on his upper lip and chin. "Do I need to shave?" he asked himself. "Ah the hell with it. Since it is a day of rest, I'll wait until tomorrow." Dressing, he decided to get something to eat. The only place within walking distance was Ben's. He would go there only if Kay wasn't working. If she were, he'd have to look for another eatery.

He climbed the diner steps and peeked in. Not seeing Kay, he thought to himself, *good, she isn't working*. He entered Ben's and took a seat at the counter. He ordered a hot roast beef sandwich so he could eat and run. He did not want to be there if Kay should show up. Gulping his food, he hoped that he wouldn't get heartburn.

As he was about to leave, he suddenly froze in his tracks. Entering the diner was the police sergeant who had picked him up earlier for fighting. He was heading his way. The officer saw John while John was trying to look the other way.

"Hey, you," he said as he reached out, grabbed John by the shoulders, and spun him around. "You're the fella who was in my jail last week, John something."

"No sir. It wasn't me," John answered, trying not to appear nervous. He looked toward the floor. "My name is George. I'm from the neighborhood."

The sergeant walked around John. "How long have you worn a moustache, George?"

"For the last six months," John replied, with a weak smile. "Why are you looking for this John something?" John asked.

"The man rode into town and started a fight in a local restaurant and beat up one of our local men. We picked him up for disturbing the peace," The sergeant answered. "I don't want trash like that coming into our town." The sergeant continued to stare at John for what seemed to be forever. "Okay, George," he finally concluded. "Sorry for the inconvenience."

John walked briskly up Derry Street with a sigh of relief. *Thank God for the moustache.* A shiver went down his back. He shuddered at the thought of being suspected. As he was crossing Oak Street, the sounding of a car horn startled him. John turned to see Kay driving the car. *My lucky day,* John thought. *First the fuckin' cop who almost recognized me, now her.*

"Are you lost, handsome?" she teased John.

He wasn't happy to see her. He wanted to forget, but there was something about Kay that made John feel happy to see her.

"No, I'm not lost," he said, as he walked around to the driver's side of the car. With elbows planted on the window ledge, he leaned forward with his face partially in the window and almost touching hers.

She was wearing a fresh, clean, uniform high above her knees, enabling John to get a full view of her thighs. Feeling his blood rush to his head, he backed off. As he moved back she noticed the growth on his upper lip and chin.

"A moustache looks good on you. It makes you look sexy. You'd look even sexier with a beard, too." She added, "I'm on my way to work. Where are you headed?"

"Just going for a walk and a breath of fresh air," John answered.

"So, how is business these days?" she asked facetiously. He said, "It's coming along and, like all new businesses, will take time," John said.

She changed the subject.

"How about getting together, say dinner at my place?" John thanked her but said, "Did you forget our agreement?"

"I mean dinner only, nothing more," she answered.

"You know as well as I do, first dinner, then showing off your sexy bod." He backed away from the car, telling her, "It was nice to see you." He continued to walk to his rooming house.

*   *   *

Hank found John lying on the bed in his skivvies, listening to opera music with a beer in his hand. "Boy, John. How can you stand that shitty music?"

"The same way you can stand listening to your shitty music." John chuckled.

*   *   *

The next morning Hal picked them up at seven-thirty. They arrived at the garage to find an elderly lady sitting in a brown station wagon. She was waiting for the garage to open for business. Hank spoke to the lady then directed her where to drive her car. He thought to himself, *why the fuck do I always end up with the old bitches, and John the young chicks?*

Luckily all she needed was a minor carburetor adjustment that he completed in fifteen minutes and for which he charged her a few bucks. She left.

Hank walked to the office and found John wearing a broad smile. He had been watching Hank from the office. John put his arm around his shoulder, "Hank, there will always be a spot reserved for you in heaven."

Hank slipped from under John's arm, ignoring him. John, Marty and Hank hurriedly donned their work clothes, anxious to begin preparing for the paint job. They washed and dried the car for the last time. Hal prepared the primer and the paint spray while the others leaned against the wall to watch him. Hal put on his facemask, closed the door, turned on the ventilating system, and the paint spraying began.

A thin primer coat doesn't require much time, so Hal was finished in no time. With the primer finished, John asked Hal how long the final coat would take.

"Several hours," he replies. "I'll have this sucker done by late afternoon."

"That's cool. Tell you what. Let's take a break. You guys relax and I'll pick up lunch." Again, John needed a breather.

He was back in forty-minutes, with enough Chinese food for a smorgasbord. They settled in the office. John gave Hal the chair as a reward. He, Marty, and Hank used the orange crates.

At one in the afternoon, Hal was ready for the big push. He painted the doors and fenders first. That way he could begin painting the insignia and car number sooner. The guys stood staring at Hal in awe.

Hal turned to John and told him, "I need the emergency rack lighting. Would you mind going to town? Find a specialty shop that carries those types of lights." He showed John a photograph as a guide.

John answered, "No problem." He turned to Hank and told him to come along. They got into the station wagon and left.

Hal decided to take a break and washed the dust from his face. Marty did the same. Suddenly, he heard a boisterous, "Hello. Anybody here?"

Hal turned his head, "Holy shit. It's Officer Goody." He quickly closed the door of the paint booth and rushed to greet him.

Seth told him, "I'm in the neighborhood making my rounds so I stopped by to say hello."

Hal thanked him and walked toward the patrol car and ran the palm of his hand across the top of the hood. "Still holding up I see," he said, referring to the wax job.

"Yes, sir. In fact, it's the best looking squad car in the precinct, thanks to you. And they think I did the work." Seth winked.

"Great! Tell you what, bring it back in three weeks, I'll wax it one more time. That should last through the winter."

Seth thanked him again. They shook hands, as Seth was ready to leave.

"Oh by the way, there is something you could do for me, Seth."

"Name it."

"A friend and me are going to a masquerade party in a few weeks and we would like to go as policemen. Do you know how to go about picking up two police uniforms?"

Seth answered, "Shoot, that's easy. There's a uniform company located at the West End Shopping Center, about fifteen miles east of town going toward the airport. It's the same company that furnishes our uniforms and there would be no problem matching ours. The only problem is, they don't rent uniforms. They only sell them."

"Great! I'll check it out." He thanked him, and Officer Goody continued his rounds.

*   *   *

John and Hank cruised around town and found the specialty supply store. He parked the car and re-styled his hair. He looked like a typical country hick. Donning his sunglasses, he told Hank to wait in the car.

As he approached the counter, John was greeted by an elderly gentleman. "Sir, what can I do for you today?"

John asked him about the rack lights.

"No, sir. Sorry, but I only carry the single and double emergency lights. Full length rack lights are a special order, and I don't know of anyplace that makes them."

"Thanks anyway, pop."

John was about to leave when the clerk said, "Say, hold on a minute. My brother has a used auto parts shop at the edge of town, and if I am not mistaken, there's a wrecked police car in his yard. Hold on a second." He picked up the telephone and called his brother. "It's still there? Good. How about the light? Okay, I have that part in stock. Okay, Frank, I am sending him over," he said as he looked at John, who nodded in concurrence.

He excused himself and went to a back room. He returned with a small box and handed it to John. "It's a small lens for one section that is missing. Replace it, and the light should be good as new. My brother is taking it apart, and it should be ready when you get there."

He gave John the directions. John thanked him for his help, paid for the lens, and added a ten-dollar tip. John left the store and went to pick up the light. At the junkyard John was about to get out of the wagon when he saw the wrecked police car parked in the far corner of the yard. He stared at the police car, thought for a second, and then turned to Hank. "Hank, check the trunk for a screwdriver." Hank momentarily stared at John with a confused expression but then got out of the station wagon. He looked for and found a screwdriver. "Perfect Hank," John said. "Now while I'm in the office picking up the light, you mosey over to the police car and remove the tags and put them on the back seat.

Hank now realized what John had in mind. "Great thinking, John. Great thinking."

While John kept the guy busy, Hank took care of the tags. With the rack light procured, John and Hank returned to the shop. Hal was hard at work completing the paint job.

"Take five, Hal. I found the light you need plus the auto tags from the police car. Check them out."

Pandemonium engulfed the room. Hal was so amazed he could not believe it. "How did you manage to pick up the exact fixture and auto tags?" Hal asked.

"I happened upon a specialty store. This old shop owner put us in touch with his brother who owns an auto graveyard, who happens to have a wrecked police car, which happened to have salvaged emergency lights."

"Wow, this is the second time we lucked out today."

"How so?" John asked.

"Officer Goody stopped by to say hello. I asked him about the uniforms. He told me we can purchase them at the West End shopping center."

"That's cool. That's the same shopping center where we picked up the paint and the equipment for the car. Funny I don't remember a uniform store. Do you, Hank?"

Hank paused and scratched his head. "Forget it, Hank. I'll work on it tomorrow."

Pleased with today's accomplishment, John called it a day, but Hal wanted to continue working for another hour or two because he wanted to apply the insignia at least on the one side.

"No way," John said.

But Hal insisted and stated that they would only be in the way. John reluctantly agreed and told him that he would pick him up at six.

"You got it, John." Hal went back to work.

*   *   *

John was on his way to pick up Hal, who was already waiting at the sidewalk. John drove him to his rooming house to shower and dress while they waited. While he was toweling off, Hal surprised John by telling him that the police car project was completed.

"Hey! Cool, Hal."

John and the guys congratulated Hal, and to celebrate, John decided to have dinner somewhere other than in town. He recalled seeing a roadside cafe a few miles from town one day on the way to the airport. It was not the greatest looking place, but the sign advertised Land and Sea dinners and he thought that he'd give it a try.

John found the cafe without a problem. They entered and were seated by a short, balding guy who was no doubt the owner. There was a circular bar to the left as they entered that sported twelve bar stools. On one side of the room there were booths, on the other side tables. The lighting could have been better. It was informal and the crowd was subdued. The food was beyond their expectations. The steak was so tender that only their forks were needed to cut it.

Afterward, John decided to relax and drink beer and shoot the bull a while. He sat back and took out his Marlboros. He smoked, drank beer, and conversed with the guys. After two hours and four cigarettes, John asked for and paid the check. He told Hal to drive. "Pick us up at eight in the morning."

*   *   *

Hal was on time, but John and Hank overslept. He had to wake them and wait as they dressed. They arrived at the shop and just settled in the office when a police car pulled into the driveway. John saw that it was Sergeant Winslow.

"Okay, Hal. Get rid of him fast."

Hal and Winslow exchanged greetings. Winslow looked around the shop and asked Hal about the lube pit.

Hal directed him to the spot and pointed to the schematic of the proposed pit location. "We didn't start yet, Sarge. As you can see, business is not exactly knocking the doors down. So we're going to wait a week or so before modifying. If business does not improve, we'll have to look for a better location."

"Good thinking . . . What's your name again?"

"Hal, Sarge. Hal."

"Right, Hal. The realtor should have told you that this place bombed out as an auto repair shop." He turned and headed toward the paint booth.

John noticed. *Shit, the bastard is walking toward the paint booth.*

"Hell, John. He'll see the police car!" Hank said nervously.

"No shit, Hank." John looked around for something to use for a weapon. Finding a twelve-inch pipe behind the filing cabinet, he grasped it in his hand. Hank looked into John's eyes and saw a look he had never seen since knowing him. It was a barbarous expression. Hank suddenly became frightened.

"You're not gonna-?"

"You bet your ass, Hank. Unless you have a better idea. I'm not having this bastard screw up my plans. This is my chance of a lifetime, and no cop is goin' to mess it up."

"B . . . b . . . but he's a policeman."

John ignored him and stared straight ahead as he gripped the pipe tightly in his right hand, moving slowly to the office door, ready to do whatever he had to do.

Hal and Winslow were in the paint booth for what seem to be forever. John's nerves were at their peak when he heard, "Okay, Hal. I hope your business picks up, and if I know anyone requiring auto repair I'll certainly recommend them to your establishment."

John was stunned. As he watched them walk toward the shop exit, Hal laughed as he waved Winslow good-bye.

I must be losing my mind. John thought. He dashed toward the paint booth, flung, the door open, and saw the Ford Taurus completely covered from top to bottom with a heavy cloth material. It fit the entire car as neat as a glove.

A look of anger spread across John's face. As Hal stood by the door smiling, John approached him with the pipe still in his hand, and raised it as though to strike Hal. After glaring at him for a few seconds, he dropped his hands to his side and the pipe fell to the floor.

"I'm sorry for not telling you, John, but I completely forgot," Hal apologized.

John was still in shock (not to mention Hank who had pissed in his trousers after watching the ordeal with the sergeant and seeing John's reaction).

Hal looked at the pipe lying on the floor. "Were you going to use that pipe for what I think you were going to use it?"

"You're right. I couldn't afford to have that bastard discover the police car. That would have been a complete give away."

"I'm glad that you were ready to take action, but I'm even happier that you didn't have to."

John picked up the pipe and underhanded it to the far corner of the shop. "Let this be a warning Hal. No more surprises. The next time I'll bash your fuckin head in . . . . By the way what possessed you to purchase the cover anyway?" As if nothing had happened, both John's mood and the subject changed quickly.

Relieved, Hal told John that it was purchased by accident. "While I was in the parts store looking around, I noticed the car covers on display. I thought it would come in handy to protect the Ford from dust and dirt, and now from Winslow."

John let it go at that. "I'm going to the shopping center to pick up the police uniforms."

He looked at Hank tilting his head to one side then the other. He paused. "Thirty-six short Hank?" John extended his arms to measure Hank's shoulders. "Yes. You're a thirty-six short." Hank just stared at John, trying to understand what he was talking about. John let it go and left for the shopping center.

*　　*　　*

John arrived at the uniform company at approximately ten. Before getting out of the station wagon he adjusted the rear view mirror so that he could change his hairstyle for a disguise. Using his comb, he parted his hair down the middle of his head; he combed his hair down the sides of his face. He looked like a typical country hick. He donned his sunglasses and entered the store.

A young female clerk in her mid-twenties, with dark shaggy hair and thick acne covering her face approached him. "Can I help you, sir?"

John added stuttering to his act and told her, "Yeyeyes, aaaaaa frfrfrfriend of mimimine and mmmmmmme ararare gogogoing to aaaaa masmasmasquerade parparparty ananand were plplplaning on gogogoing as popopoliceman and would llllllike tototoo rent twtwtwo popopoliceman uniuniuniforms for thrthrthree days." John was playing dumb, as Hal had already told him that they only sold the uniforms. He did such a good job with his hairstyle and the stuttering that the clerk turned her head and laughed. She apologized and said, "I'm sorry sir. I just thought of something funny that happened to me this morning."

John just nodded and thought, *That's okay, bitch. I'm going to have the last laugh.*

As expected, she told him that they did not rent but only sold the uniforms. John

Asked, "Whawhawhat issss theeeee cooost?" Almost bursting into laughter again she answered, "Fifty dollars. The accessories are an additional ten dollars."

John paused, as though thinking about it, which worked out perfectly.

Feeling sorry for laughing, she changed the price to fifty dollars for everything. John agreed and gave her the two sizes. She placed the uniforms in a plastic bag. John paid her, thanked her, and turned and walked out of the shop. He head toward the station wagon with a grin that spread from ear to ear, humming all the way. He took his comb and restyled his hair back to its original look.

*   *   *

It was no surprise that John found the guys playing cards. As usual Marty was losing. John walked to where the Ford was parked. He returned and asked Hal, "When will you install emergency lights?"

"Not until the morning of the heist, John. Installing the lights now would only make it difficult to cover the entire car, due to the additional height the lights would create. You never know when Winslow would show up."

"That's cool, Hal." John suddenly thought about the utility company. "Okay, Hal it's time for you to check out the utility company. First thing in the morning using the telephone book, look for the utility company location. When you find it, go there and look over the area. There could possibly be a diner or bar in the vicinity of the plant where employees gather to shoot the breeze. If there is a bar or diner, mingle with the crowd and see what type and color uniforms they wear. You must accomplish this mission without allowing anyone to become suspicious. Understood?"

"No sweat, John," Hal said with confidence.

*   *   *

John decided to have dinner at the roadside cafe again. The food was as good as the last time. However, this time, the steaks were much larger. In fact, they were so big that neither of them could finish the entire meal. However, Hank being Hank asked for a doggie bag.

Hank recommended a nightcap of beer at Ben's. "What do yea' say John? Just for a little while."

As much as John wanted to say no, he thought maybe they should relax a little; he approved, hoping that Kay had the night off. Lady luck was indeed on John's side this night, for Kay was not working. They sat at their usual table at the far corner of the diner and ordered a round and shot the bull as they sipped their beer.

John glanced at his watch. "Okay, guys! Time to hit the road." The first stop was John's rooming house. He and Hank got out. John told Hal, "Pick us up at eight thirty at the intersection of Oak Street because the nosey landlady gets up in the morning.

*   *   *

Hal arrived at the intersection and picked up John and Hank exactly at eight thirty. Hal stopped for coffee to go. Arriving at the shop they sat and drank their coffee. John told them that all was going well and that he was going to the bank to have a look around. "Nine o'clock, Hal. Let's get moving. If you don't mind, I'll drive the station wagon and you drive the truck," John said.

Hal knew that whether he minded or not, he was using the truck. So he answered, "No problem, John," and they were on their way to complete their mission.

*   *   *

The bank was unusually crowded. The line being long, John had to wait ten minutes for his turn. It was just as well, since it gave him additional time to survey the building and the bank personnel's traits.

Finally, he heard the teller Mr. Jackson say, "Yes sir, Can I help you?"

Funny, John thought, *Marty was right when he told me that I never got in line with a female teller.* As usual he had ended up with none other than "Mr. Personality"—Jackson. This guy had a disposition that would not quit. John placed his ID card and deposit box key on the counter. He signed the access card. Jackson took the key and led John to the vault area. Jackson took the box from the shelf and was about to hand it to John, when he said, "My, this box feels as though it's empty."

John lost his control. He snatched the box from his hand. "You writing a book?"

Startled, Jackson backed off. John quickly took hold of him self and apologized. This was not the time to act up. He took the box and hurried to the booth. He closed the curtain part way and began surveying the bank's interior. As always from that location, the only position he could see was the tellers and the front entrance.

He eliminated the teller since they always worked in the same position. He did notice that the guard's ass was glued to a stool approximately three yards from the entrance of the bank. He looked for but could not see the manager's location from his vantage point, so he put that off until he returned the deposit box. He estimated the distance from the entrance of the bank to the teller position to be approximately 200 feet, which he jotted down in his notebook. He got back in line to return the deposit box to a teller.

As he stood waiting in line, he could feel Jackson's eyes fixed on him. He looked toward the manager's desk and estimated the distance between the bank entrance and his desk to be approximately ten to twelve yards, and again he jotted those figures in his notebook. He looked toward the guard whose ass was still glued to the stool. This told John that he would be easy to find as they entered the bank when the heist began. Finally, he was able to return the deposit box.

He turned and walked slowly out of the bank to the parking lot and the station wagon. He leaned back in the seat, took out his pack of Marlboros, and lit up. He relaxed for ten minutes. He took out his notebook and drew a small diagram of the bank. After studying the diagram, John laughed. *Just like I figured. The heist should take approximately nine minutes and change.*

Suddenly, he stopped laughing and seriously thought. *The utility company plan has to work. Otherwise we're dead.* John shook his head. He started the engine and left.

*   *   *

In the meantime, with the help of the phone book yellow pages, Hal found the utility company located at the edge of town. Across the street from the utility company Hal saw a sign for Peg's Bar and Grill. It was a small, antiquated place with a mahogany bar and worn, brown industrial carpeting on the floor. It attracted a large crowd made up mostly of workers from the utility company. Hal glanced at his watch and guessed that this had to be the midnight shift just ending.

The uniform of the day was orange rubber suits and coats with orange helmets. There were a few white helmets scattered about, who were probably supervisors. Hal managed to get a stool at the far corner of the bar and noticed that almost everyone was drinking booze. A small percentage were having the usual bacon and eggs. So he too ordered a drink. Of course it was too early for him, but he had to fit in. After the first swallow, he decided to have breakfast instead.

He tried striking up a conversation with the guy sitting next to him. "Tough night?"

The guy looked at Hal without uttering a word. Hal quickly extended his arm to the barkeeper and pointed to the drink the guy was consuming. The barkeeper refilled his glass. The guy took a swallow. "It's always tough on the graveyard shift. Thanks for the shot, uh, uh—"

"George. You're welcome," Hal answered. The guy introduced himself as Frank. Hal felt that he had the right guy; however, he seemed to have a hollow leg. He was into Hal for four drinks in only thirty minutes. It was fortunate that Hal had extra money with him. Frank asked him what he was up to. Hal answered that he was looking for a job and thought about checking with the utility company.

"Not a chance. They're laying off fifty workers the first of the month," Frank answered. Hal paused and thanked him for the information. Hal looked for and saw the utility worker's identification badge clipped on his upper right shirt pocket. He pointed to it and said, "Everyone wears an ID badge over there?"

"Required by the company. Allows employees access to certain work areas." He unclipped the ID and handed it to Hal for him to look at. After examining it, Hal placed it on the bar. Hal did not take his focus from the badge. He waited for Frank to take a long swallow of his drink. When he did, Hal, using his finger tips, flipped the badge up his coat sleeve. Slowly, he placed his hand in his coat pocket and shook his sleeve until the badge fell into his pocket.

By this time Frank was flying high, so Hal took advantage of the situation by telling him he liked his work clothes and would not mind owning a set.

Frank looked at Hal for a second or two, then, in a slurred voice, told him, "The only place you can purchase a set is at the plant employee's store, and only employees are allowed to make purchases." He leaned forward to get Hal's ear and whispered, "If you meet me here at ten o'clock on Friday morning, I'll pick up a set for you for a hundred and fifty dollars."

"Great! I'll be here at ten Friday." Hal thanked him again and said that he had to get going and find himself a job. He was off to the shop.

*   *   *

Hal arrived at the shop to find Hank and Marty playing cards. Marty was bitching at Hank, saying he was not dealing the cards fast enough. "Aw, fuck you, Marty," Hank answered back.

John return from the bank. He turned to Hal and asked., "How did you make out?"

"Great, John, great!" He furnished John the complete details. "All I have to do is replace Frank's photo with mine and I'm set."

"I only hope that the bank manager buys your story and does not verify the temporary shutdown with the utility company or the police," John said.

Hal agreed, and then told John that he would find a photo shop in town after lunch. John was sitting on the only chair and Hal was on the one crate, Hank on the other. Marty bitched that a business should have decent chairs for people to sit in.

John immediately agreed and directed his attention to Hal. He winked. "Hal, when you go into town for your photo, pick up six chairs." He turned to Marty and asked, "Any particular style or color Marty?"

"Funny, John. Really funny."

John gave Hank money to pick up a case of beer. Hank was back in twenty minutes. They sat drinking beer. To retain their confidence, John told them that all was going great thus far and further explained to Marty and Hank Hal's success that morning with the utility company employee.

He turned to Hal and said, "Since you're going to play the part of a utility worker, you'll require the necessary equipment. When you're in town for your photograph, check with a heavy equipment company about renting a cherry picker, the type lineman use. You'll need it in order to go through the motions of repairing the overhead wires, providing the bank manager doesn't check with the utility company or the police. If he does, we abort the heist, and go back to the drawing board."

Marty happened to mentioned the excitement of speeding through the road block with siren blasting and lights flashing . . .

"Shit, John. Shit." Hal was upset.

John was stunned. "What's the problem?"

"The siren. We forgot the siren!"

"It's my fault. Tell you what: you take the station wagon. I'll take the truck to the junk-yard and hope that the wrecked police car is still there." John took his beer in hand, got into the truck, restyled his hair again, and put on his sunglasses and headed for the junkyard.

John arrived at the junkyard and walked briskly to the location where the police car was previously parked. He turned in disgust when he did not see it. He happened to glance to the right and saw it parked under a heavy metal crusher, about to be crushed to the size of a pancake. He ran toward the crusher shouting as loud as he could for the operator to stop, as the hammer was being prepared for the kill. John was too late. The hammer came crashing down and the police car was gone. John turned away and thought that things had really been going great until now. Again he cursed himself for not thinking about the siren.

The owner who saw John and his crazy antics came running out. "What the hell's wrong with you, mister? Trying to commit suicide? Say! You're the volunteer fireman who bought the rack lights."

John answered that he was, and then he explained about requiring the siren to go along with the lights.

"No problem," The owner said.

"What do you mean no problem?"

"You don't think that I'd be that stupid as to demolish a wreck without completely stripping it of all usable parts?"

"You mean you still have the siren?" John asked.

"Sure do, in the parts room."

John let out a sigh of relief as they walked to the parts room.

"It's expensive," the owner said.

"Name it," John answered.

"A hundred and seventy-five dollars."

John did not flinch. He drew out his billfold, handed over two one hundred dollar bills, and did not wait for his change or sales receipt. He put the siren in the truck and returned to the shop.

*   *   *

Hal was already back with the forged identification badge. John told him that the siren was on the seat of the truck and then asked about the equipment. "No sweat, John. The equipment company charged eighty dollars a day rental and only one day notice is required," Hal said.

"That's cool Hal. Good work." John walked to the office. Marty and Hank were fast asleep. John laughed. He watched Hal pick up the siren from the truck and went to the paint booth to install it.

Hank's snoring was annoying John, so he walked to the paint booth and watched Hal install the siren. Hal completed the job in an hour and was ready to test it. John told him to hold on a second. "I want to go to the office before you do the test. I want to see Marty and Hank's reaction to the blast." Hal waited until John gave him the signal. When the signal came, Hal turned on the siren switch. "Vaaaarrroooom"! sounded the siren.

Surrounded by concrete walls, the shriek was deafening. Marty did not react at all, but Hank scrambled with panic and bounced off the wall and fell on the floor. Hal came running. They laughed as Hank massaged his head and cursed John for not warning him of the test. "That's what you get for sleeping on company time," he told him.

"Aw, balls to you, John." Hank again massaged his head. Marty just stared at the three of them as if nothing happened.

John sat down at the desk. "Okay listen up. We're set for the heist with the exception of the weapons that I'll concentrate on tonight. I'll call Sid in Chicago for a possible contact in Cincinnati, which is only a hundred miles or so from Worthington. I'm still thinking of ways of beating the alarm system. Until then we'll go with Hal turning off the alarm for repairs. I still have a gut feeling that the bank manager will question the shut off and check with the utility company or the police. But that's the chance we'll have to take. Most importantly, we have to keep an eye out for that fuckin' Sergeant Winslow. He could show up at any time. If and when he does, we need to explain to him that business isn't getting any better even with the customers he's sending us, so we'll have to look for a new area. Hal, make certain that the police car is covered at all times."

"No sweat," Hal answered.

John then decided to go over the heist procedure.

"The night before the heist, we'll place the station wagon at an abandoned service station that I located on the same road toward the airport. It sits in 50 yards from the road, approximately four miles out of town. It's perfect.

"I'll buy a used car on the day before the heist. We'll use the car for the trip to the bank for the heist, then return to the shop and pick up the police car. We'll abandon the used car on a side street. After we beat the roadblock we drive directly to the abandoned station and ditch the police car. Then we get into the station wagon and our getaway.

"This is how the heist will go down. The day before the heist I'll drive Hal to pick up the cherry picker. Twenty minutes prior to the heist Hal will drive the cherry picker to the bank. We'll follow Hal with me driving the getaway car. I'll park within a block of the bank. Hal will park the cherry picker on the sidewalk and enter the bank. If the manager cooperates, Hal will exit the bank and set up the cherry picker. That will tell me that the heist is a go.

"I will then drive to and park by the bank with the motor running. Hank, you will enter the bank first and take the bank guard. Marty, you follow Hank and go directly to where the bank manager is seated and put your gun to his head. I'll be behind Marty, and I'll go directly to the tellers' location and collect the money and leave the bank. The entire heist and return to the shop should take approximately nine minutes and forty seconds.

"Hal, soon as you set up the cherry picker, go directly to the car and the driver's side. Keep the motor running and be ready to roll when we exit the bank. At the shop we transfer the money to the police car. Hank and me will change into police uniforms. I'll be driving, Hank will be riding shotgun. Marty, you'll be laying on the floor."

John paused. He turned to Hal and said, "Hal, you will be in the trunk, then we head out of town with sirens blasting and lights flashing. We get by the roadblock, and we're home free. Any questions?"

"I have one, John. What if the manager does not cooperate?"

"Good question, Hal. If it's a no go, you exit the bank and walk toward our car. We'll drive back to the shop and check out our alternatives. Any other questions?" There were none. "Good. Marty, you and Hal are on your own for dinner."

*　　*　　*

John was first in the shower. Afterward, he relaxed in the bed with a beer and his opera. Hank put tissue in his ears so as not to hear what he described as shitty music. John's rest was short-lived because he had Sid Green and the weapons on his mind, so he dressed as Hank finished his shower. They finally left for dinner.

*　　*　　*

In the meantime, Marty and Hal freshened up and left their rooming house for dinner. Marty said that he would drive, and, sure enough, he drove to Ben's Diner.

Kay was on duty. She hurried to where they were seated. When she arrived, she looked toward the door.

"He's not coming. He's busy tonight, but I'm here," Marty said with a smile.

"Thanks loads," she answered. She took their order and walked toward the kitchen. Marty's eyes followed her every movement.

Hal was getting itchy and not enjoying his meal at all. In fact, he ate so fast it gave him heartburn. When Kay returned to clear the table she bent over and Marty patted her butt. She backed off and let loose with a left hook across Marty's jaw that just about took his head off. He fell off the chair to the floor.

As if that wasn't bad enough, a policeman sitting at the counter having his dinner heard the commotion and walked over. He took Marty by the arm, sat him down, and reached for his radio to call for a police wagon.

Hal looked at Kay. "For John's sake," he whispered.

She paused, stared into Hal's eyes, then told the officer, "It's okay, Willie, just a little misunderstanding."

"Are you sure, Kay?" Willie asked.

She answered yes and thanked Willie, who went back to his dinner. Hal thanked Kay and, without a check, he gave her twenty dollars and rushed Marty from the diner to the truck.

"Wow, she packs a mean punch," Marty said, rubbing his jaw as he got into the truck.

Hal looked straight ahead not saying a word. Marty knew that Hal was upset, but he could care less.

*   *   *

Hank enjoyed his meal of Yankee post roast followed by an ice cream sundae. John finished his roast beef. Instead of dessert he opted for a cup of coffee. Then he and Hank had an after-dinner drink.

John looked at his watch and thought that Sid should be at the deli. He told Hank to stand by and have another drink. He would return after he called Sid about the weapons.

John managed to get change from the cashier. He looked for and found a public phone on the sidewalk outside the restaurant so that he could speak freely without anyone listening.

After the usual greetings, John explained that they would probably use his recommendation of having someone impersonate a utility worker.

"You're taking a hell of a chance, John, but you never know, it could work. What else can I do to help?"

"Four pistols, .357 magnum, if possible. If not, whatever I can get. With Cincinnati close by, I figured you may have connections in that area." Sid answered that he did not, but he had a friend who did. He asked John to call him before lunch tomorrow.

John returned to the restaurant and finished his drink. Hank had already finished his drink. John paid the check and went home.

*   *   *

John and Hank enjoyed the extra hour of sleep. In fact, they had time for a sit-down breakfast. They later arrived at the shop to find Marty under a jacked-up car cursing. Hal was on his knees with tools in hand assisting Marty by handing him the tools, as he needed them. He looked at John and just shook his head.

"What's this all about?" John asked.

"Guess," Hal answered.

"That damn Winslow again, drumming up business for us."

"You got it, John."

Marty pushed himself out from under the car and looked up at John. "A band adjustment on the transmission, and I'm having a problem with it."

"What do you think, Hank, can you help him?"

Hank paused, scratching his head. "I'll give it a shot." He joined Marty under the car. There was silence, a grunt, silence, and two more grunts. "You got it," Hank shouted. "Now let's check it out."

They pushed themselves out from under the car. Marty slammed the hood down and got in the car. He was about to start the engine when a police car pulled up onto the sidewalk. Yes, it was none other than Sergeant Winslow again. John took Hank by the arm and headed for the office. He told Hal, "Thank him and tell him that we don't need his help anymore, and that we are closing shop because business was that bad."

Winslow greeted them as Marty started the engine and took it for a test drive. Hal returned Winslow's greeting and explained that Marty was road testing the car to check out the transmission. He thanked him for the business.

"No problem. Eh, what's your name again?"

"For the hundredth time, Sarge, it's Hal."

"Right, Hal," Winslow said as he looked around. "Business still bad, I see."

"It's so bad that we'll probably close shop in a few days and look for a new location," Hal said.

"I don't blame you." Winslow walked toward the office. John and Hank hid under the desk so as not to be seen. Fortunately, Marty returned to the shop and parked the car, saying, "Good as new. Good as new."

That altered Winslow's course toward the car. He paused and took a last look around shop, bid his farewell, and left. John walked from the office. "We lucked out, again. This is the last straw." John was really pissed. "After that car is picked up, lock the friggin' doors and don't open up for any one. We're out of business as of now. We use this place for meetings only until the day of the heist."

After regaining his temper, John said, "Okay, let's keep things rolling." He turned to Hank and directed him to visit the realtor tomorrow and inform him that they would vacate the building a week from Friday, heist or no heist." Hank looked at John with a puzzled look. "That's the day after the heist, John!"

John looked at him. "No shit. Do you want to tell him that we're vacating on Thursday so that he can put his lock on the door? Then we have no access to the police car after the heist."

Hank blushed and said that he would see the realtor first thing in the morning.

"Hal," John continued, "I want you to put up an Out of Business sign on the door now!"

"Sure, John. Right away," Hal said. John went out to find a coin phone and called Sid about the weapons.

*　　*　　*

Again Sid answered the phone and greeted John. "I have good news, and I have bad news, John. How do you want it?"

"It makes no difference Sid."

"Well the good news is that I found the weapons. Four .357 magnums. The bad news is that they're only available in Cleveland."

"That's about two-hundred and fifty miles." John was upset. "Well, at least we'll have the weapons. Thanks, Sid. Where and how much?"

Sid furnished the location first. "A small tavern on the south side at 112 South Putnum Street. It's called Barrels Cafe. Make certain that you go south Putnum, not north. You ask for Barrels. He's short, fat, and ugly." Sid laughed. "Tell him you were sent by Gino Puglese to pick up the iron. The cost is twenty-five hundred dollars. I know that's a little high, John, but Gino gets his cut."

"I understand, Sid. Thanks, again I owe you."

CHAPTER 7

John forgot to close the garage door, which allowed a car to drive into the shop. The car was driven by none other then Kay. John cursed himself for not closing the door. Hal noticed that it was Kay, and he turned to Marty who looked like he was about to have a heart attack.

John walked to the car and greeted her. She poked her face out of the window. "Hi. I just happened to be in the neighborhood so I thought I'd stop by to see how you and your business were doing."

Bullshit, John thought.

She looked around the empty shop. "You look like you are doing fine, handsome, but your business looks anemic."

"You were right on target when you told me about an auto shop not surviving at this location. I'm thinking about closing and relocating to another town," John replied.

Marty was a little on edge thinking that Kay might tell John about the incident at the diner, and he wished that she would hurry and leave. To make matters worse, she waved at the guys before turning her attention back to John. "I saw you at the bank the other day. You were taking notes."

"Just checking my finances," John answered.

"Or maybe planning a bank robbery?" She answered coyly.

"What gave you that idea?" John asked, beginning to get angry. "Let me remind you that you were the one who said that the bank could be not be taken. In fact, you called me insane."

"There's always a first time for everything," she answered.

Now, really angry, he stared at her brown eyes. "What do you want from me, Kay?"

"You, just you and nothing more. Before you remind me about our agreement, I'll remind you that I'm not looking for a husband. All I'm asking is, give me just a little of your time. After that I don't care if you rob Fort Knox. When you're ready to leave town, you leave. That simple." She stared into John's eyes.

John paused as suddenly an idea crossed his mind. He should take her to a motel and murder her, eliminating the possibility of her snitching after the robbery.

"Tell you what. I'll meet you early next Tuesday morning. We'll find a nice motel and spend the entire day and night wining and dining and making love. One thing, though. We have to be back Wednesday not later than noon."

Kay's eyes lit up. "Why wait for Tuesday?" she asked puzzled.

"I have a lot to accomplish in the next few days," John answered. She stared into is eyes, paused, and agreed. "We'll have to use your car. Pick me up at the shop Tuesday at nine," John told her.

"No problem," she answered excitedly. "I'll tell my boss today that I'll be taking a two days' vacation." She started the car. "Until Tuesday."

John nodded and smiled. She backed out of the shop and drove off.

John walked slowly and deliberately to the office. He sat down on the orange crate.

"What did she want John?" Marty asked.

"All she wanted was to see how business was going. So I told her that every thing was going good."

Marty was relieved and happy that she hadn't said anything.

Good ole' Hank, with his mind in the gutter, said, "What else did she ask for, John? What else?"

"Do you want me to tell you that she wanted to have sex with me, Hank?" John answered.

"Well, did she? Did she?" John just stared at him and smiled. The others joined in with the laughter.

"Now for the business at hand," John continued. "I contacted Sid regarding the weapons, and he came through. Four .357 magnums. The only problem is, if you want to call it a problem, that the weapons have to be picked up in Cleveland. That's you, Hal. Hank will ride shotgun. You will leave at approximately nine in the morning, using the station wagon. If all goes well it should take eight to ten hours for the entire trip. You have two options. If you're too tired to drive, Hank could take over. The second option is that you can sleep over at a motel and return the next day. It's entirely your decision."

"Gottcha, John." Hal answered.

John gave Hal the requested cash plus expenses money. John reached in his coat pocket for a sheet of paper that contained the information and address of the bar in Cleveland, including the contact's name. He gave it to Hal and told him to make certain not to lose it."

*　　*　　*

Afterward, John decided to take a walk for a breath of fresh air, to clear his mind and think out the heist plans. Before realizing it, he had walked almost ten blocks. He returned to the shop to find the guys playing cards. He sat and watched and drank beer. Hank was winning all the money and Marty was bitching as usual. John looked at Marty and said, "If you can't take losing, you shouldn't gamble."

"Screw you, John," Marty answered.

John laughed and glanced at his watch. "Okay, guys, let's call it a day and go have dinner."

After dinner, they sat around with after-dinner drinks. After a few drinks they left for their living quarters. Hank fell off to sleep. John, however, lay on the bed listening to his aria. He became restless, tossing and turning. He sat up at the edge of the bed and checked the time. It was ten o'clock. "Hank, you awake?"

Hank answered, "If I wasn't awake then, I am now." Hank was startled when John told him to dress and be ready to go out for a bite and a drink. Before John could finish the sentence, Hank was dressed and ready to go.

Arty's Bar and Grille was near empty for this particular night of the week. John and Hank picked a booth at the far corner. They ordered beef sandwiches and beer. They ate and drank at a leisurely pace as they watched two couples on the dance floor. Hank looked around for a loose woman, and to his disappointment the pickings were slim to none. John saw the disappointment in Hank's eyes. "Maybe a few broads will show up soon. Hank."

"Sure, when the place closes for the night." Hank was pissed. John was rolling his glass between the palms of his hand hands when suddenly he heard a familiar voice from the booth behind them. He looked at Hank and put his finger to his mouth to signal him not to speak so that he could listen. Ear cocked, he tried to match the face with the voice.

"I'll be a son of a bitch. That's Jackson the teller from the bank," he whispered. Then he heard, "Look Jackson, I could care less about your wife being sick and all your friggin' problems. You're into me for twenty-five grand. You had your friggin' fun with the young chick. Now you must pay the piper. I'll give you one week from today to pay off what you owe, including ten percent interest, or all hell will break loose. It's your ass. Your wife will take what's left of your ass when I tell her about your romance with the young chick."

John stared at Hank and vice versa. John whispered to Hank with a smile. "There's the solution to the bank alarm system! With his help I can put Hal back into my original plan."

"How can you be sure that he'll play ball, John?"

"I'm sure. In fact, I'm positive. I've seen guys in his situation many, many times before.

At that moment, a huge, burly man who seemed to be ten-feet tall stood up, stared at John with a nasty look, and left. John stood up with a grin, turned toward the next booth, and said, "Hello Mr. Jackson."

Jackson stared at John. "The safe deposit box, four eighty three."

"You got it, Mr. Jackson." John signaled to the barkeeper and pointed to "Mr. Jackson.

"Scotch on the rocks, and make it a double . . ." John ordered a refill for himself and Hank as well. He allowed Jackson to take a few sips, then turned to him and said, "I understand that you have a problem. A one week and twenty-five thousand dollar problem."

"Well you understood wrong. I have no problem," Jackson stuttered.

Disregarding his statement, John said, "I'm certain that I can be of some help to you. In fact, I know I can help you solve your problem."

"Sure, fairy godfathers, eh?" Jackson answered mockingly.

John became furious but managed to control his temper. "That's a piss poor way of appreciating friends who are willing to bail you out of your crisis, Mr. Jackson," he said, forcing a smile. "I said I can help you, and it won't cost you a dime."

Mr. Jackson stared at him. "Okay. I'm listening, but there has to be a rational reason for your wanting to help me."

"Meet me at my auto shop tomorrow at five and I'll explain my reason." John jotted down the shop's address on a napkin. He gave it to Jackson. "At that time, I'll explain how I can help you with your problem."

"Sure, I'll be there. Five o'clock." Jackson said.

John and Hank finished their drinks. John placed a twenty-dollar bill on the table. John left with Hank in hot pursuit. Jackson appeared bewildered. He sat with eyes fixed straight ahead.

On the way home, Hank asked John, "Do you really think that you can trust him?"

"I'm sure; in fact, I'm positive. I've seen guys in his situation, many times before.

*   *   *

The next morning John didn't hear Hank leave for his trip to Cleveland to pick up the weapons.

John picked Marty up at ten-fifteen. On the way to the shop they stopped for breakfast. John told Marty about the previous night's encounter with Jackson. Marty was impressed but skeptical. He asked John the same question that Hank had asked him: "Can this Mr. Jackson be trusted?"

"Trust me, Marty. We have here an opportunity to solve the alarm situation . . ."

*   *   *

On highway seventy, Hal was making good time. The road sign read, "Cleveland 22 miles." Hal turned to Hank. "What do you think,

Hank? Is that fast or is that fast? We should complete this trip in only four hours, including stopping for breakfast and two piss stops to boot."

"Right on, right on," Hank shouted.

At the Cleveland city limits, Hal stopped at a service station for fuel and directions to Putnam Street. With a fill-up and directions, they continued on their way.

They finally arrived at 112 Putnam Street, but there was no Barrels Tavern in sight. Hal checked and rechecked the paper. "I don't understand, Hank. That's 112 on the corner, but it's a grocery store."

Hank took the paper from Hal's hand and checked it. "You're right, that's what it sez, 112 Putnam," he said panning the area.

Hal circled the block a second time as he drove slowly. He happened to look in the rearview mirror to see a police car following close behind. Without turning his head, Hal informed Hank.

"Oh, shit," Hank said.

Hal told him not to look back but to look straight ahead and not show any panic. "Check the glove compartment for Marty's registration, Hank." Hank checked the glove box. "No. No registration," Hank stuttered.

"It has to be there. Keep looking!"

Frantically, Hank took everything from the glove box and placed it on his lap. He went through the entire contents. Nothing. As a last ditch effort he ran his hand around the glove box. Sure enough, he found the registration wedged in the corner.

"Got it Hal! Got it! Whoeeeee!" Hank yelled.

By that time, there was a quick burst from the siren and blinking lights. The police pulled Hal over to the curb.

"I'll do all the talking. Don't say anything unless the policemen ask you questions. Understood?"

"Gottcha."

One policeman approached the station wagon, as the other stayed in the car using the radio, no doubt checking on the station wagon.

"Good afternoon, gentleman. How are we doing today?" he said as he craned his neck to look in the back seat.

"Just fine, officer," Hal answered.

The officer looked at Hank, who was sitting up straight as if frozen, staring through the windshield. The officer then turned his attention back to Hal.

"May I see your registration and driver's license, please?" Again he looked at Hank, and then he looked at the card. "You're a little way from home," the officer said as he walked back to the police car with the registration in hand.

He returned and stared at Hal for a second and asked him, "What brings you to Cleveland?" Again he stretched his neck to look in and around the back seat.

"My sister moved to Cleveland a year ago and I'm visiting her for the first time. She's expecting me today. The only problem, officer, is that she supposedly lives on 112 Putnam Street. But that address turned out to be a grocery store."

The policeman thought a moment and said, "What's the address again?"

"112 Putnam Street," Hal repeated.

The policeman paused, then he laughed out loud.

Oh shit, what's he laughing about! Hal thought to himself.

The officer stuck his head in the window, "You're probably looking for the south side. You're on the north side of Putnam Street."

Relieved, Hal and Hank chimed in with laughter. The officer gave Hal directions to South Putnam Street. Hal thanked him and drove on. Hal looked at Hank. "Why didn't you tell me south instead of north? You could have gotten us locked up," Hal joked.

"Me?" yelled Hank. "Blame the fucking boss. He didn't say beans about north or south."

"Only kidding, Hank," Hal said.

Finally they reached Barrels Tavern. Hal parked and they got out to stretch after the long ride. They entered the crowded tavern, which was noisy and very smoky. It was a typical neighborhood tavern. The bar itself was made of frosted glass blocks through which multicolor lighting showed. It was about forty feet long with a dark-stained wooden top. There were at least twenty dark brown padded wooden bar stools and six wooden tables.

As Hal and Hank stood at the entrance, every face in the crowd resembled the FBI's ten most wanted fugitives. They were about to approach the bar when they encountered a big brawny guy well over six-foot who was no doubt the bouncer.

"What can I do for you?" His breath was something else. Hal almost passed out from the putrid odor. Hal was going to ask him what brand of mouthwash he used but thought better of it.

Hal turned his head to avoid direct contact with him. "I'm looking for Barrels."

"Yea, what makes you think he's here?"

Hal was about to answer when a short, fat, balding man waved to Hal, motioning him to his table.

"I'm Barrels. What can I do for you?"

Hal looked at the four other men sitting at the same table who seemed fresh from a rogue's gallery.

"That's okay, you can speak here," Barrels said.

"Gino Puglese sent me." Hal answered.

Barrels motioned to the others to leave. He invited Hal and Hank to have a seat.

"What about Gino?" Barrels asked.

"I was sent by Gino to pick up the iron," Hal said.

He offered Hal and Hank a drink, motioning to the barkeeper who took their order of two beers.

"Have lunch yet?" Barrels asked Hal.

"Come to think of it, we haven't," Hal answered.

"Good. I want you to taste a veal that is unlike anything you will ever taste again in your lifetime." He sent word to the kitchen. He could not have described the veal better, for the flavor was beyond Hal's expectation. It was so tasty that Hank had two servings.

Barrels had a carton brought in and handed it to Hal. Hal gave Barrels the money. Barrels escorted them to the door and shook their hands.

Hal looked at the bouncer, laughed, and whispered to Barrels, "That guy should change his brand of mouthwash."

Barrels laughed so hard that the sound seemed to shake the entire building.

The bouncer figured Hal was talking about him, but before he got to the door, Hal already had the package in the trunk and drove off.

*　　*　　*

Back at the shop at five-fifteen Mr. Jackson was a no-show. Marty looked at John. "I think you drew a blank, John."

Ignoring his remark, John just continued relaxing and staring into space.

At precisely five-twenty a car drove into the shop with Jackson behind the wheel. John looked at Marty. "There's your fuckin' blank, Marty." I'll do the talking. I don't want this guy upset anymore than he may already be."

"Hello, Mr. Jackson." John introduced Marty and they walked back to the office. John offered Jackson the chair. John and Marty sat on the wooden crates.

"Okay, Mr. Jackson. I'll come right to the point. You're into some punk for twenty-five grand. I'm going to pay off that debt for you and give you a bonus of an additional fifty-grand. In return, you perform a service for me."

"What service can I perform for you? I have nothing to offer," Jackson protested.

"You work at the bank, correct?"

"So?" Jackson answered.

"As a bank employee you know the layout of the entire building including the alarm system."

Jackson stared long and hard at John. "You're thinking about robbing the bank? Mister, whoever you are, you're out of your skull. It would take Houdini to rob that fortress."

"Jackson, I'm not asking your opinion. I'm making you a decent offer."

"I do have a choice. I'll take my chances with Sanders."

"How about your wife?" John stared at Jackson with a confident grin.

"I'll take my chances with my wife also." Jackson nervously cracked his knuckles.

"Your decision, Mr. Jackson. Remember. Forget what you heard and saw here tonight or you and your wife will no longer have *any* problems. Is that clear?"

"Quite clear," he said as he rose from the chair and began walking toward his car.

Marty stood up and prepared to go after Jackson. John took him by the arm. "John, you have to be kidding. He's got us over a barrel."

"Patience is the name of the game, Marty. That's why I'm in command of this operation."

Jackson's car engine never started. He turned and walked deliberately back to the office. "Okay, okay. I'm afraid you win. What do I have to do?"

"First sit and have a drink." John took a bottle of scotch from the desk drawer. "Marty, a glass for Mr. Jackson."

"Sorry, we only have paper cups," Marty said. That brought a smile from John and Jackson.

Jackson took the cup in his hand and asked for water for a chaser. He polished off the first drink with one swallow and swished it down with the water. John refilled his cup.

"Now tell me, Mr. Jackson, how the fuck did you get involved with this hood, I mean, loan shark, for twenty-five grand?"

"Would you believe it if I told you that a hard-on got the best of me?"

"Sure I would. I know many men in the same boat," John said as he stared at Marty.

"Balls to you, John."

John smiled. "If the shoe fits, Marty." John felt being funny on purpose might make Jackson relax. "I'm sorry, please continue." Apparently it worked, as Jackson now appeared to be relaxed.

"In my type of job you meet all kinds of people, and Sheila is one of that kind. She had all the necessary tools to drive any man up a wall. Just twenty years old, five-foot seven inches tall, hair black as coal, with the bluest eyes you'll ever see. Thirty-four, twenty-eight, thirty-four with legs to match! You would have to see her for yourself."

"You mean there's a broad like that in this town?"

"Go on please, Mr. Jackson." John glared at Marty.

"Sheila always made certain to bank at my window. She would eye me in the sexiest ways. Well, being fifty and all, I told myself that I had nothing she wanted and I played it off. That was all well and good, until one day she asked me if I would buy her a drink after work. Well, gentlemen, this was the beginning of the end for me."

"Wow! Then what?" Marty asked.

"Give him a chance, Marty. Give him a refill," John said.

After a pause and a sip of scotch, Jackson continued, "Well, I was like a kid on my first date. She began telling me how distinguished I looked and that I only appeared to be in my forties. The irony of it all is that I was eating it up. I wanted to believe her. Before you know it, I was taking her out to dinner."

Marty interjected, "But how does that amount to twenty-five G's?"

"Hell, man, I'm just warming up. Now she's on her way to really snowing me under. I gave her a hint about a little love after dinner at her place. She told me that she could not take me home because of her father being a drunk and her mother being sickly (and the fact that she lived in a slum area). I told her that we could go to a motel. She said that motels made her feel uncomfortable and that she would really like to move to a decent place of her own. Then she could invite me over, and we could have a good time and all that bullshit."

John, was confused. "What were you doing meanwhile, like having sex?"

"Well, until she could find a place of her own, she would satisfy me by letting me fondle her and put my hand up her dress. To keep me interested, she would throw in a bonus, and fondle me but with my trousers on. I finally got tired of that. I wanted to get into her pants really badly. So, I took what little savings that I had from my knockdown money and got her a pad of her own. I finally got a chance to throw it to her. Man, she was good. However, she was shrewd. She had a limit.

"She gave me just enough to keep me paying the bills. As your friend here says, she had me by the balls. This continued for a couple of months, and then she told me that she needed new clothes so she could look sexy for me. The dinners and clubs became more frequent. My savings finally ran dry, and I was at the point of no return. I thought about telling my wife, but she has a bad heart. Of course she would have killed me."

John tried his best not to laugh but couldn't help it. He excused himself and went to the bathroom. When he returned, he told Jackson to continue.

"Well, I played the entire ballgame. Meanwhile, she was getting more headaches. You know what that means. As I mentioned, my funds were zero. So I thought about embezzling. As I said earlier, that bank is tough. I'd get caught in a week. I happened to be talking with a friend of mine and casually mentioned loans. He told me he knew some guy who made loans to people by lending five dollars with a six-dollar return. At the time, it sounded great to me, so my friend referred me to Mr. Sanders, a loan shark if you will. Every five dollars you borrowed there is a return of six dollars. Twelve for ten and finally the big, leagues. Hundreds lead to thousands. The interest alone was something else. See this scar?"

He pointed to a spot above his right eye. "That's just for missing two payments. As I said earlier, when the hard-on gets the best of you, forget it!"

John started to feel sorry for this guy, which was unusual for him.

"How long was this so-called relationship going on?" Marty asked.

"About six months," Jackson answered. "She strung me along as long as I came through with the nice things: money for the rent, nice clothes. Of course her headaches were becoming more frequent. Now she was beginning to get greedy and began asking for more money. That's when he turned my head toward the wall."

"When what, Mr. Jackson?" John asked.

"I generally work at the bank Wednesday evenings to make extra money for myself. This particular Wednesday I didn't feel up to working, so I begged off and headed home. Instead, of going home I decided to stop at a neighborhood bar for a nightcap. I entered the bar and there she was sitting in a booth with a young man. Fortunately her back was turned toward me, so she didn't see me. I sat in the next booth so that I could listen to their conversation.

"That's when I heard, 'Hey, Sheila, when are you going to hit the old guy for some more loot? My funds are getting low.' And she said, 'In time honey, the guy doesn't own the bank; he only works there.' The guy growled at her and said, 'If you can't come up with more bread by this Thursday I'm cutting out, understand?' She begged him not to leave and said that she would see me that week and ask for more money. To top it off, she told him that she could not stand being touched by me and called me a scumbag. She pleaded for him to take her home and make love to her."

"That son-of-a-bitch," Marty said. "Then what?"

"I stood up and confronted her. She was shocked to see me, especially when she realized that I had heard the entire conversation. She tried to explain that she was only kidding. I called her a slut. That's when the young guy punched me out. Fortunately, the bouncer booted him out. She took off like a bat out of hell. That ended the relationship."

John looked at him and asked, "Do you still see her?"

Jackson answered, "She comes to the bank now and then but she stays clear of me. I hear that she was playing some department store manager, the poor bastard."

"You have some story, Mr. Jackson." John tried to show him sympathy. "You help us, and I'll see that you get back on your feet."

Mr. Jackson paused and looked at John, then at Marty, picked up his empty cup, and asked Marty for a refill. In fact, he asked him to fill it to the brim, and he put it away in one gulp. He didn't bother with a water chaser. He asked John when and how he was going to rob the bank and what his part was in the robbery.

"A week from Thursday at approximately 12:45, using the routine stick-up. Explain the alarm system."

"It's a silent alarm," Jackson answered.

John took this opportunity to check if the electric company scheme might work. So John explained method to Jackson.

Jackson laughed. "No, it won't work. The bank manager would verify it with the utility company after notifying the police."

"Now, explain the silent alarm system," John asked Jackson.

"Each teller has a button located on the floor by their feet. There is also a switch under the manager's desk."

"The million-dollar question, Jackson: Is there a central cutoff switch? If so, where is it located?"

"Yes, the main switch is mounted on the wall behind the tellers," Jackson said.

John rubbed his hands together. "Now I'll explain your role in the heist. At exactly, 12:44 you deactivate the switch. We enter the bank at 12:45. We complete the heist. You immediately reactivate the switch after we leave. This will be easy due to all the mass confusion that we'll create."

Mr. Jackson interrupted John, "This would not give you enough time to evade the road block."

"No problem. That's all worked out. You just take care of the alarm after we're gone."

"You know that I'll be taking a big risk, and I don't know if the risk is worth seventy-five thousand, considering that you are looking at a minimum of two million dollars."

John stared at Jackson for a moment, "I'll tell you this, Mr. Jackson, you learn fast."

"Like I said earlier, it's going to be tough. So I might as well know how much my chances are worth," Jackson said with a smile.

"Jackson, I have to admit that I agree with you. How about two hundred and fifty-thousand?"

Jackson looked at John, trying to search out his bottom line. Failing to do so and realizing that this was going to be his final offer, he thought for a minute, took a final sip from his drink, and accepted the offer. He then asked John, "How and when will the payoff be made?"

"I'll leave your share somewhere in the shop after the heist. The location will be decided at our final meeting next Wednesday at five."

Jackson looked at John with a sheepish grin.

John understood his facial expression. "You will have to trust me as I will have to trust you, Mr. Jackson. Furthermore, you can identify me to the police as the thief."

It sounded logical to Jackson, and he stood and shook John's hand. "I'll see you Wednesday at five."

John noticed that Marty's face had skepticism written all over it when Jackson left. "We have no choice but to trust Jackson. If he does pull a double-cross, he's dead."

"Okay, I hope you're right," Marty answered.

John looked at his watch. The time was seven-thirty. He asked Marty about supper. Marty replied that he was starved. They got into the truck and headed for town. Marty recommended Chinese food. John agreed and found the same restaurant where he had picked up lunch before. The restaurant was decorated in the typical Chinese motif, with orange walls trimmed in black and multi-colored crepe paper lanterns. The aroma of Chinese vegetables boiling in the kitchen greeted them.

They finished their meal with an after-dinner drink. John looked at his watch and wondered if the guys were back or had decided to stay in Cleveland. John asked for and paid the check. They were on their way to Marty's rooming house. John turned to Marty and said, "If Hal is back, he is to secure the weapons at your place overnight, then take them to the shop in the morning. One more thing, Marty. Since we are out of business, there is no need to be there at eight o'clock. So I'll pick you up at ten."

"You got it, John," Marty answered.

*   *   *

When he arrived at home, John found Hank already in bed with earphones in place, listening to country-western music and reading the newspaper at the same time. John sat beside Hank. He lifted one earphone from his ear.

"How did the trip go?"

"A piece of cake. We were back by nine o'clock and had supper on the way back." Hank kidded John about his screwy directions to Putnum Street.

"Shit. I completely forgot to mention east, west, north, or south to Hal!" John laughed. John then told Hank about his chance meeting with Mr. Jackson, who would provide the solution to the alarm problem.

"So the utility plan never would have worked?" Hank asked.

"No, but we've got a better plan now. Jackson will take care of the alarm before, during, and after the heist, allowing us enough time to complete the job."

*   *   *

Everyone arrived at the shop at ten o'clock. John immediately noticed the sign that Hal had painted: "Closed until further notice." John then told Marty and Hank to park the truck and station wagon inside the shop. As Hank drove the truck into the shop, John felt hungry for breakfast. He approached the truck and gave Hank money to pick up bacon and egg sandwiches and coffee. He also told Hank to signal with two short blasts of the horn upon his return. "Close and lock the fuckin' door, Hal," John said.

Hal closed and locked the door and joined John and Marty in the shop office. "I forgot to bring the weapons and ammunition to the shop, John. I have them stashed in the room, secured."

"No good, Hal. I want those weapons here at the shop. I want this accomplished today. Understood?"

"Understood," Hal answered.

John went on to fill Hal in on the development involving Mr. Jackson. "We're back to our original plan. You won't have to play the role of the utility company employee."

Hal looked at John with disappointment. "Heck, John, I was looking forward to acting the part." Again Hal looked directly at John and was about to speak.

"Mr. Jackson will have to be trusted, Hal."

Hal looked at John with amazement. "How did you know I was going to ask you that?"

"Marty and Hank asked the same questions. I figured you'd join the crowd."

Finishing his coffee, John leaned back, took out his pack of Marlboros, took a cigarette, and lit up. He looked at the three of them and asked, "None of you guys smoke these cancer sticks?"

He got a "no" from all three.

"You guys don't know what you're missing. That's why I'm always calm, cool, and collected," he said, grinning. He took a long drag and exhaled. John stared at Hank. "What about your mission today, Hank?" Hank looked at John puzzled. "The realtor, Hank, the realtor."

"Sure, sure I remember." Hank blushed as the others laughed. John took out the lease he had filed in the desk drawer. He handed it to Hank and reminded him to tell the realtor that they would be out by Friday. "You think that you can remember that without forgetting, Hank?"

Upset, Hank took off for the realtor.

John looked around the shop, and his eyes stopped and focused on the paint booth. "When was the last time you started the Ford?" he asked Hal.

"I don't remember," Hal said, surprised. "I'll do it right now." He hurried to the Ford.

John smiled bitterly when it took Hal several cranks to get the car started. "You see, Hal you must start the car at least once every day so that it will be ready Thursday."

Hal assured John that from now until the heist, he would start it up twice a day.

John wasn't through yet. "How about gas?"

Hal checked the gas gauge. "Just shy of a full tank, John."

"That's cool. Now that the shop is closed for business, keep the door locked at all times. Repeat: keep the door locked no matter what. We'll continue using the two short horn blasts as a signal to enter the shop."

At that moment, a car horn sounded. It was Hank returning from the Realtor's office.

"So how did it go with Mr. Twinkle toes?"

"Great, John. Except he's sending someone Friday to inspect the building for missing equipment or damage. He also requested that someone be here."

"Sure, we'll be here in a pig's ass," John said robustly. "We'll get rid of the crates and clean the place Wednesday. I'll have to arrange to return the key to Twinkle Toes somehow."

John looked at the three of them and said, "We have a money problem. My funds are down to the bare minimum. I don't have enough money to buy the getaway car, and so, I have to return to Chicago for additional funds to get us through the balance of our stay. We still have to eat and we need money for miscellaneous requirements, unless you guys have some loose money stashed away that would save me a trip back."

John held his breath. Marty answered first, "I have a total of thirty dollars, John." Hal and Hank dug through their pockets and came up with a total of forty bucks.

"Not even close," John answered. "I'll leave in the morning. I should be back sometime Wednesday. Meanwhile, we move from our room's Wednesday. Bring our bags here to the shop, and spend the night here at the shop."

"You mean sleep here Wednesday night?" Marty asked.

"You got it, Marty. You don't expect to check out of your room Thursday morning, then rush to get here and go for the heist. Just say that you can't check out Thursday morning, then what . . . ? I admit that it will be a little uncomfortable, but for one night we'll survive," John said.

He gave Hal money and told him to pick up a few blankets. "Between the car that I'll purchase Wednesday and the bed of the truck, it wouldn't be that bad. He turned his attention to Hank and explained, "I'll tell the landlady tonight, and then all I have to do is turn in the key Wednesday morning. She may want to inspect the room. That will be my responsibility. I'll make sure that the room is clean and in order."

"Any other questions?" John asked. There were no takers. "Okay, then you guys are on your own until Wednesday. Remember we have a final meeting with Mr. Jackson at five, Wednesday evening. One more thing. Trouble. Don't get yourselves in any trouble, particularly with the law, understood?" All three nodded. Hal drove John and Hank to their rooming house. John reminded Hal that the weapons were to be brought to the shop today.

"Practically done, John," Hal said.

Later that day, John knocked on the landlady's door, but there was no answer. He waited and knocked again. John looked at Hank. "She must be out shopping."

In their room Hank jumped in bed, put on his earphones, and tuned in county-western music. John sat on his chair by the window and gazed onto the street. He was relieved that all had gone well and that there were no questions concerning his trip.

John looked at Hank who seemed to be asleep. He walked over to make sure that he was asleep. He walked out quietly and walked to Ben's to have a cup of coffee and check with Kay about their trip.

Kay was on duty as he had hoped. He sat at the counter and ordered a cup of coffee. "I'm set and ready to go," she said.

"Fine, I would appreciate it if you were to pick me up a block from the diner instead of the shop."

"No problem." She smiled and continued waiting on a customer.

He drank his coffee and returned to his rooming house. He lucked out a second time that day, for the landlady was outside sweeping the sidewalk.

"Good afternoon." *Shit, I don't even know her name*, he thought.

She acknowledged his greeting anyway. "Good afternoon to you, Mr. London."

John went on to tell her that he was moving from his rooming house Wednesday. She stared at him for a second or two. "Anything wrong with the room?" she asked.

"To the contrary, the room is perfect. However, my business failed to materialize, so I'm moving back to California."

"I'm sorry to see you leave, Mr. London. I wish you the best."

"Thank you. I'll return your keys Wednesday morning."

He decided to pack his suitcase and garment bag that day rather than wait until morning.

*   *   *

Hal stopped for Marty on his way to pick up John and Hank. He arrived at John's rooming house at six-thirty. In fact, they were waiting for him curbside. Marty suggested Ben's.

"Go for it, Hal," John said. The guys were shocked to hear John agree so quickly. Of course, John knew that Kay would not be there.

They sat at their usual table at the far corner. Marty's eyes spanned the entire diner looking for Kay. Not seeing her, he focused his eyes toward the kitchen, thinking that she may be placing an order; however, no Kay. Instead, a short, skinny waitress attended to them. "Hi fellas, my name is Jane and I will be your server. What will it be?" John ordered a round of beers first, then he, Hank, and Hal placed their orders. She turned to Marty who seemed to be in a trance and asked, "Sir, do you wish something to eat or are you just drinking?"

Marty regained his senses and said, "I'll have the same." The waitress stared at Marty. "You'll have an open face roast beef sandwich, pork and sauerkraut, and Yankee pot roast, all at the same time?"

Embarrassed, Marty looked at her and said, "Make it a hamburger, fries, and beer."

All three stared at Marty and smiled. But good ole Hank had to make a comment: "Marty you look like you're in the twilight zone."

"Ah, Fuck you, Hank," Marty said angrily.

"Just kidding with you, Marty, just kidding." They topped off their meal with desert and coffee. Then John decided to sit awhile, drink beer, and shoot the breeze, which caught the guys by surprise, but it was a happy surprise. John took out his pack of Marlboros, stuffed a cigarette in his mouth, lit up, and began puffing away. The guys talked about girls, their stay in prison, and told sexy jokes.

Suddenly, a thought crossed John's mind. It would be better for him and Hank to check out of their room Tuesday instead of Wednesday to save time. "Hank, take your belongings to Marty's place and shack up there Tuesday evening. Hal, you pick Hank up at eight-thirty Tuesday morning. I'll clean the room and make certain that the furniture is properly placed in its original state. I'll return the keys to the landlady Tuesday morning. That'll be one less detail to be concerned about. Any questions?"

With no takers John called it a night. "You guys can stay awhile longer if you want. I'll walk home." The guys elected to stay.

After John left, Marty ordered another round. With Kay transfixing his mind, he would not be satisfied until he found out her whereabouts.

When the waitress returned with the drinks, Marty asked, "Say, I don't see the other waitress, what's her name?"

"You mean Kay? Oh no. She was on earlier in the day." She placed their drinks on the table. Marty stared at his glass of beer and then smiled as he realized the reason John agreed to eating at Ben's. He had known all along that she would not be working.

Hal noticed Marty's weird facial expression and asked him if there was something bothering him.

"Nothing, nothing at all. Just thought of something funny," Marty answered.

*   *   *

John was in bed listening to opera music. He began to doze off when Hank returned, his words and actions revealing that he had had a little too much to drink: "Still listening to the fucked-up music, eh John?" he asked as he walked to his bed and sat at the edge to begin undressing.

John completely ignored him and lowered the volume. "If you aren't too drunk to understand, Hank, remember to take your belongings in the morning."

Hank mumbled a few words and fell asleep. John shook his head, turned off the radio and fell asleep.

To John's surprise, he awoke to the sound of Hank taking a shower. He reached for his watch and found the time to be seven-thirty. He turned on his back and stared at the ceiling. He thought of two more days and the possibility of being a millionaire and doing all the things he had thought of doing while in that rotten prison.

His thoughts were interrupted as Hank returned from the bathroom.

"Good morning, John. Sorry if I woke you," he said as he dried his hair with a towel.

"No problem Hank. I was already awake." John suddenly noticed Hank's beard. "The beard. Better shave it."

"But, I was just getting used to it. Besides I like it."

John reminded him that he would be wearing a policeman's uniform Thursday. "Cops normally do not have beards."

Hank looked at him. "You're right." He marched back to the bathroom. Ten minutes later he returned without the beard.

John managed a smile. *Hank was right; he did look better with a beard*, John thought. "An improvement, anyway." He smiled again.

"You laughing at me?" Hank asked John.

"Me? I wouldn't dream of laughing at you."

Hank finished dressing and converted his bed back to a sofa. He packed his bags and placed them by the door. He looked at his watch. It was eight-fifteen. Hank told John that he was going down to the sidewalk to wait for Hal.

Hank picked up his bags. As Hank was about to leave, John noticed that he was wearing baggy trousers. An idea sprouted in John's mind: coveralls. "Hold on. I just got an idea that would reduce the time between you and me changing into police uniforms when we return from the heist. We'll wear coveralls over our police uniforms during the heist. When we return to the shop, we strip off our coveralls. Presto, police uniforms, saving at least ten minutes before we head for the road block."

Hank stared at John with his head tilted to one side. He was puzzled.

"Never mind, Hank." John reached for his billfold and took out twenty dollars and gave it to Hank with instructions to have Hal pick up two sets of coveralls. "My size is forty long. You, Hank, your size is thirty-six short," he said, jotting the sizes on a slip of paper. He gave Hank the money and the paper. Hank put the money and paper in his pocket. John turned on the radio and listened to music as he started tidying up the entire apartment, which included rearranging the furniture.

*   *   *

Hank reached the sidewalk just as Hal pulled up, but Hal did not stop. He kept driving on. Hank wondered what was wrong as Hal circled the block. This time Hank stood in the middle of the street so Hal had to stop. Hal stuck his head out the car window.

"Hank? Holy shit. What happened to you? I didn't recognize you."

"Hell, all I did was shave my beard," Hank said.

As Hal drove off, he asked Hank, "Why did you shave your beard?"

"John told me that the police don't wear beards."

Hank didn't see Marty and asked Hal, "What about Marty?"

"He's taking a shower, I'm on my way to pick him up now," Hal said.

Marty was waiting curbside when Hal arrived. Marty suggested breakfast and, of course, he suggested Ben's. He would not rest until he saw Kay. Hank and Hal agreed to Ben's, and Hal turned to Marty and reminded him not to make the same mistake as he had the other night. Marty did not answer. Hal turned the car around and drove to Ben's. They went to their usual table. Marty had his eyes focused on the kitchen. To his surprise, only one waitress was working the tables, and it was not Kay. They placed the same order of eggs over easy and bacon.

"Hey, sweetie, is Kay working today?" Marty eyeballed the waitress.

"No. Kay's took the next two days off."

Marty thanked her.

"You're not going to win, Marty. Why not just give up on it?" Hal said.

"Mind your own business, Hal." Marty glared at Hal. Before things got out of hand, Hank was smart enough to intervene; as a distraction, he told Hal about John ordering that they get coveralls as he gave Hal the money and slip of paper.

Again Hal was impressed with John's thinking. They finished their breakfasts and set out to purchase the coveralls.

*   *   *

Finished shaving, John dabbed after-shave cologne on his face. He checked the time: ten-forty. He picked up his luggage and garment bag and closed and locked the door. He checked the door a second time to make certain that it was locked. He went down the stairs and saw that the Landlady was already outdoors hosing down and sweeping the sidewalk. She greeted John.

Returning her greeting, John handed her the keys. "Would you like to inspect the room before I leave?"

"No. It won't be necessary. I'm sure that you left it in good order." She wished him well and continued cleaning the sidewalk.

She wasn't really all that bad, John thought. He was now ready to meet Kay. Arriving at the rendezvous area, he found Kay waiting. He approached the car, greeted her, and put his suitcase and garment bag on the back seat. He got in the passenger's side. Kay drove off, heading out of town. She looked beautiful. Her face was exquisitely made up; her blouse was cut low and her skirt was drawn half-way up her thighs.

"Are there nice motels within driving distance?" John asked.

"Yes," she answered. "There is a lake resort located thirty miles past the city limits. It does not officially open until Memorial Day weekend. But the motel is operational including the dining room. I called ahead for reservations."

"Cool. It appears that you did your homework," John said.

The drive lasted approximately fifty minutes. Kay took the scenic route.

The driveway leading to the motel was long and winding, with a water fountain and a row of towering oak trees that stood like soldiers. It had a country club atmosphere. Once they reached the front entrance, John got out of the car and went in to register.

With the key in hand, John found their room. The door opened to a luxuriously decorated, elongated room that resembled a bridal suite, complete with a king-size bed and end tables that dominated the entire wall. The matching end tables held huge lamps and a Bible. A television was housed in an off-centered armoire. Elegant tapestry draped the windows.

After unpacking, Kay sat on the edge of the bed for a breather, her legs fully exposed. The two stared seductively into each other's eyes, and then she immediately became the aggressor. She removed his tie, unbuttoned his shirt, and unbuckled his belt. His trousers fell to the floor and formed a puddle around his feet.

He had become spellbound and confused by her assertiveness. He wasn't used to women being the aggressors. She totally undressed him, and then she removed her clothes: first the blouse; there was no bra to remove. She dropped her skirt to the floor and stepped out of it. With outstretched hands, she pulled John onto the bed. He landed on top of her and then he succumbed to her desires. He lost all sense of control. Their hearts were ablaze.

He held her head in his strong hands; his fingers webbed through her long brunette tresses, which were no longer clamped in place with a huge barrette. His hot breath was all over her lips, her neck, up and down her cheeks; he nibbled on one breast and then the other. He arched his body as he plunged into her.

She felt secure in his embrace. As they lay entwined like vines, she ran her hands up and down his chiseled physique. Her screams of ecstasy were earsplitting.

*   *   *

They walked to nearby Adolph's restaurant for a light snack and stopped at the sign that read, "Wait to be seated." The maitre'd introduced their waiter, who coincidentally was also Adolph. They started with drinks; she had a martini on the rocks and he had a bourbon and ginger on the rocks.

She swirled her mid-afternoon martini and plucked the olive from the glass. He smiled as he watched her put the olive in her mouth and lick her fingers. They sipped their drinks slowly as they studied the menu. He shook a cigarette from its pack and lit up. "Do you mind if I smoke?"

"Sometimes. When there isn't good ventilation."

He rested the cigarette in one of the notches of a crystal ashtray as they placed their orders. After a light snack of soup, chef's salad, and wheat toast, she looked intently at him eating his food.

Afterward, they walked out into the cool, early summer breeze and breathed in the clean, fresh air. They strolled leisurely along paved paths that lead to a lake about fifty yards from the restaurant. The weeping willow trees danced in the light wind in time with the rhythm of the birds' chirping. They hardly noticed a groundskeeper scooping up petals and dead flower heads from an early bloom. The bluebird of happiness sprinkled a bit of horny dust on Kay and she wanted to return to their room. As their eyes sucked in the magnificence of the entire area, he thought, "One could easily get lost at this resort."

"A penny for your thoughts," she said, giving him a long, sexy look.

"Nothing in particular. I'm just enjoying the scenery."

"Shall we return to the room?"

Reading her suggestive look, he asked, "You mean now?"

"Of course. Why not? You said we were going to love each other to death. Didn't you?"

He smiled as she took him by the arm and led him along the path that led back to the motel rooms. There in their room they carried out their sexual encounters many times in several different ways.

*   *   *

Their table at Adolph's was ready when they arrived for dinner. John glanced around the restaurant and was pleased that there weren't too many other people there. He had wanted to keep a low profile until the heist. They ordered their favorite pre-dinner drinks: she her martini and he his bourbon and ginger.

When the waiter with the same name as the restaurant returned with his order pad, Kay made up for her light lunch. She began with crabmeat-stuffed mushrooms and then added onion soup topped with melted cheese and a six-ounce prime rib. He ordered shrimp cocktail and lobster with all the trimmings. While they were eating, they heard music coming from the next room. There was a combo playing in the lounge; they continued drinking and dancing cheek-to-cheek until closing time.

Once they had returned to their room, John undressed down to his shorts. He turned on the radio to a music station and lay on the bed with his arms folded behind his head, staring at the ceiling as though in deep thought.

Kay returned from the bathroom dressed in her lace gown and heels; it was enough to get a reaction from John. She approached him and immediately got on top of him, and so the torrid lovemaking began.

There sex act completed, Kay immediately fell off to sleep. It was time to carry out his plan of disposing of Kay so that there wasn't a chance of her ever turning him in to the police in the event the reward was inviting to her. He grasped the pillow with both hands. He was about to place it over her face to smother her. But it never happened; as he stared into her face, he was over-taken by her beauty. He felt warmth throughout his body. He then thought that beside being beautiful, she had treated him with . . . John couldn't come up with the exact words. He smiled, placed the pillow behind his head, and fell off to sleep. Had John finally met his match? Or was he just mellowing?

*   *   *

The music from the clock radio blasted John's ears. He rose to a sitting position, Kay didn't flinch. The clock showed seven a.m. He retreated to the bathroom. When he returned, Kay was waiting with open arms. He stared at her and laughed.

"Not again," he said in disbelief.

Smiling she nodded her head, inviting John to charge her. That he did.

When all was done John checked out of the hotel and they were on their way back to Worthington. Kay was all smiles. John was feeling pretty good himself. On the way he spotted a used car lot. He asked Kay to drop him off so that he could look and possibly buy a car and said that she could continue on to Worthington.

"Are you sure you don't want me to wait?" she asked.

"No. I'll be fine. Thanks."

With one hand on the door handle, John leaned over and kissed Kay and thanked her for a great time.

"My pleasure," she purred.

John exited the car and stood as Kay started the car. As she drove off, John shook his head and said, "Wow! Two more days with her would have killed me."

It took John exactly one hour to purchase a used car and start back toward Worthington. On his way, he stopped at the shopping center and picked up four pairs of latex gloves to be used to wipe fingerprints from everything—and that meant everything—before the heist.

*   *   *

John drove up to the shop using the two-horn signal. Hank opened the door and John navigated his car to the far end of the shop. Hal was already sitting in the office when John walked in and sat down. He noticed the coveralls on the desk. He picked out the pair for himself and tossed the second set to Hank. He looked for but did not see the blankets. He looked at Hal.

"They're in the station wagon." Hal said.

"Cool. Now it's time to get the police car ready. Afterward I'll go to the bank and check what the midday traffic looks like."

John noticed Marty staring at him, which made him feel uncomfortable. He gave Hank money to pick up a six-pack or two. Hal closed the door after Hank, and then climbed up to the loft to fetch the emergency lights.

John turned and looked at Marty, "Okay, what's on your mind?"

"I don't know, but it seems mighty strange that you went to Chicago for more money and the waitress took a short vacation at the same time."

John glared at Marty. "First, it's none of your fuckin' business what I do. I'm in charge of this project. You do what I say, not what I do. Finally, if you don't like what I say or do, you can get into your station wagon and head back to Chicago. I can pull this heist off with three people just as well as with four."

Marty walked away without answering. Hal was speechless. John noticed and decided to help him with the emergency lights. They laid the lights on the floor by the Ford.

Hank returned with the beer. They settled down to relax. When the beer break was over, John and Hal went back to the Ford to complete the job of installing the lights.

With the lights installed, Hal began the wiring between the light and the switch. When he was finished, he turned on the lights, and they worked perfectly.

Remembering John's instructions, Hal cranked up the car and let the engine run for a minute or two before driving it back into the paint booth. He took a rag and wiped the entire car, removing the dust that had accumulated while it had been parked in the paint booth.

It was time for John's trip to the bank to check the twelve to twelve-fifteen traffic. Arriving at the parking lot at approximately eleven-fifty, he found the lot practically empty except for a few cars that no doubt belonged to bank personnel. He waited until twelve, at which time he slowly entered the bank and walked to the counter that displayed bank slips, saving account applications, and credit cards. As he pretended to fill out various forms, he was surprised but happy to observe only two customers in the bank until well past twelve-twenty. Satisfied, he turned and eased himself out of the bank and returned to the shop.

The guys were busy playing cards. They immediately stopped their game and converged on John for his report. "Perfect. Absolutely perfect." John beamed. "Only two customers between twelve and twelve-twenty. Let's hope for the same tomorrow. It being the middle of the week and month, the old bastards have no pension checks to cash."

The guys cheered and continued with their card game. John walked to the Ford for a final look. He sat in the driver's seat to familiarize himself with the car's operating controls since he would be driving.

Familiarization completed, he went back to office and told them to relax until Mr. Jackson showed up. He did not have to tell Hank a second time. He dropped the cards, picked up a blanket, went to the truck, and got in the back for a nap. Marty and Hal followed suit and settled in the station wagon. John sat at the desk. He took out a cigarette and lit up. He blew the smoke toward the ceiling and finally dropped the cigarette to the floor and crushed it with his shoe. He recounted the entire heist plan in his mind, making certain he covered every detail. He dozed off with his feet propped up on the desk.

Marty and Hal awakened him as they entered the office. "That was a quick nap," John said.

"Have you checked your watch lately, John?" Marty asked.

"No, but I will now, if it makes you happy, Marty. It's five twenty-five. So what?"

"No Jackson yet," Marty said, grinning.

"Don't worry your little ol' ass about it, Marty. Jackson will be here," John said, now getting pissed.

*   *   *

Five forty-five. John sat with his feet propped on the desk without showing any emotion. Hal could not understand how John could just sit there without at least doubting Jackson's sincerity. Marty had a look on his face that seemed to say he wouldn't mind if Jackson didn't show up, even if it meant forfeiting the money, just so he could see John fall flat on his face. But Marty's grin soon turned to a frown when a car horn sounded. John got up slowly, turned off all the lights, walked to the door, and peeked though a crack of the doorframe. When he saw that it was Jackson, he opened the door. Jackson drove into the shop. John lowered and locked the door. He walked past Marty, ignoring him completely and going directly to the office with Jackson close behind.

John sat on the chair and offered the wooden crate to Jackson. He took a bottle of scotch from the desk drawer and asked Hal to fill a cup with water for Jackson to use as a chaser. He handed Jackson the bottle and told him to pour for himself. Jackson thanked him and filled his cup four fingers high and then downed it with one swallow. He took the cup of water from Hal and finished off the first round. He refilled his cup again; only this time he nursed the second round.

He now appeared relaxed, so John began his briefing. "Your part in the heist will be easy, Mr. Jackson. First off, do you smoke?" John asked.

"A chain smoker," Jackson confessed.

"Good. At approximately 12:44, if there are no problems, you deactivate the alarm; you come out to the front of the bank, light up, and signal me that the heist is a go. You return to your station like nothing is about to happen. Am I getting through to you, Mr. Jackson?" John asked.

"Yes, sir," he answered.

"Cool," John said. "Now, if you have a problem deactivating the alarm, you will not light up, thus signaling me that the heist is a 'no go.' The heist will be aborted, and we'll meet here at the shop at five and discuss our next move."

"Cool," Jackson said as he took another sip of his scotch.

"If the heist goes without a hitch, we leave and you immediately activate the alarm switch and go about your business. Be sure to act upset like the other employees will probably be." John paused for a second. "Any questions, Mr . . . . Say what the hell is your first name anyway? I'm getting tired of calling you Mr. Jackson."

"George," he answered.

"Okay, George it is. Again, are there any questions?"

"None except when, how, and where do I pick up my share of the money?"

"Good questions. The money will be placed somewhere in the shop." John paused and looked around to determine where to hide the money. After thinking a minute or so, He turned to Hal and asked, "Is there a carton available?"

"There are a few cartons in the loft."

"That's it," John said. They walked toward the loft. John climbed up the ladder first and Jackson followed. John found a carton. "I'll put the money in this carton, and place it in this spot." Jackson seemed satisfied.

They returned to the office and John continued. "The shop door will be unlocked. You will pick up the money anytime after one o'clock." John had a spontaneous thought: he should have Jackson returned the key to the realtor. "Would you mind doing me a small favor?" John asked.

"Not at all," Jackson said, somewhat surprised.

"The key to the shop must be returned to the realtor Friday. If you were to return it for me, it would save time and a problem. I'll place the key in the box with the money." John jotted the realtor's address on a piece of scrap paper. "You can drop the key in the mail slot and be on your way with all your troubles behind you."

Jackson took a sip from his drink and stared at John.

"I'm reading your mind again, George. Is this son of a bitch going to screw me?" John smiled.

"As a matter of fact, I was thinking just that. With the exception of son-of-a-bitch." Jackson grinned.

He reminded him of their previous meeting. "You know my true identity and could turn me in to the police. Why would I risk losing the fun of enjoying my money if you were to turn me in?"

Jackson didn't answer. He finished his drink and glanced at his watch. "I'd better be getting home." He shook everyone's hands; he turned to John and said, "How are you going to beat the road block with so little time?"

"That's my problem, George," John answered.

*   *   *

John stared at them curiously. "No one hungry? I don't hear any complaints about dinner."

They looked at each other. Hank looked at John and said, "Christ, John, you mean that I'm missing dinner? I gotta be crazy."

"I'll drink to that, Hank."

John turned to Marty and said, "Okay, Marty, as planned we'll place the station wagon at the abandoned service station tonight on our way to dinner. We then can use the truck and the getaway car for sleeping tonight. We'll take the truck first thing in the morning."

Marty wasn't to keen about parking his car overnight but kept it to himself since he had already screwed up once that day.

"I'll drive the other car, and Marty will follow me in the station wagon and park. Then we'll have dinner."

John suddenly stopped talking and put his finger to his mouth a sign that they should not speak. He walked slowly toward the shop door. The guys followed close behind. One voice became distinct. It was the voice of Sergeant Winslow speaking with someone. John peeked through a crack in the doorframe and saw that it was Winslow and another police officer.

Winslow spoke, "It's a shame that the shop did not work out for those poor fellas." He tried the door, making certain that it was locked.

"Well, if Al Bonski couldn't make the auto repair business work here, what made those guys think that they could?"

"You have a point there, Jim," Winslow answered.

"Well, Harry, I'd like to stay and bullshit with you, but I have to make my rounds. If you want to guard this door all night be my guest. As for me, I have to get going. My next patrol in this area is ten o'clock. See ya, Harry,"

"Sure, see you, Jim." Winslow tried the door one more time. Satisfied, he also drove away.

John stood and listened for a few seconds, until he felt assured that Winslow was gone. He told them that every two hours on the even hour, they must check the area during the night. This meant that if they had to go out, it must be done on the odd hour. He said they must deliver the station wagon, eat, and be back at the shop by nine-forty five. "Let's get going."

Twenty minutes later, they arrived at the service station. The area was pitch-black. They used the headlights from John's car to actually see where they were parking. John guided Marty behind the building where they secured the wagon. Hank said it was so dark that it was spooky. They all got in John's car and drove to have dinner.

They finished the entire meal in fifty minutes. John paid the check.

Before driving to the shop, John drove the escape route, which turned out to be rather easy. It took only ten minutes to drive the entire route from the bank. He now arrived at the shop and drove up the driveway. "Ah, fuck!" he yelled. "I must have left my billfold at the restaurant. You guys go ahead. I'm going back to get it. I'll signal when I return." John let them out and returned to the restaurant.

Marty's eyes followed the car's taillights until they disappeared in the darkness. Hal closed and locked the door. They went to the shop office and sat, each taking a beer. Marty was the first to speak.

"I don't know about you guys, but I'm starting to wonder about John. I mean, if he can be trusted or not."

"You're crazy, Marty. Your problem is good old jealousy," Hank said, angry.

"Okay, okay. Don't say I never told you so," Marty said as he took another sip of beer.

*　　*　　*

John returned at ten-twenty and explained that he had gotten back late because he allowed a twenty-minute cushion to make certain that the police had completed their scheduled rounds. They all turned in for the night, except for John, who couldn't sleep, so he went over the entire heist and studied the map.

CHAPTER 8

D-day. John was the first to wake and glanced at his watch. It was seven o'clock. He stretched the kinks from his back and legs. He opened his suitcase, took out his toilet article kit, and went to the men's room to wash up. Afterward he put his suitcase and garment bag on the front seat of the truck.

In the meantime, the others woke up. All three made a mad dash for the men's room, which only accommodated one person. Marty, with toilet kit in hand, won the race and had the first crack at getting washed. Hal and Hank stood by staring at each other like two boxers anticipating each other's next move, working to gain an advantage when Marty finished.

Meanwhile, Hal and Hank failed to notice John leaning against the office wall laughing. "You guys missed your vocation. You should have been comedians."

Hank appeared the most comical. He wore red and white checkered boxer shorts down to his knees. However, he had the last laugh because he noticed Marty coming out and beat Hal for a turn at the sink. Marty was bitching about having to shave with cold water that caused facial burns.

He received no sympathy from John.

Hank surprised Hal by only taking ten minutes to wash. Hal followed, did his thing, and returned to the office.

At eight o'clock, John told them that if everyone was dressed and ready, they would take the truck to the abandoned service station before having a hearty breakfast. "Then we'll return to the shop, clean up, straighten the garage out, and finalize the preparation for the heist."

Then the commands began. "Hal, put the wooden crates in the truck. We'll dump them behind the service station. Before we leave, everyone place their suitcases in my car and transfer them to the station wagon when we arrive. Hal, you drive the truck. Marty and Hank will ride with me."

Crates and luggage stowed in the vehicles, they were ready to leave. John checked his watch before Hank opened the door. "Nine-thirty. The coast should be clear, but look outside for any signs of police anyway, Hank."

Hank slowly opened the door and looked in both directions. He waved John out. Hal followed in the truck. Hank secured the door and jumped into the car. They drove to the service station with John leading the way.

They had traveled a total of four blocks when John looked in the rear view mirror to see a police car with lights flashing pull Hal to the curb.

"Fuck. It's the law signaling Hal to pull over." John pulled off to the side of the intersection. His eyes fixed on Hal as the police officer approached the truck. It seemed that he was there forever. John broke out in a sweat. Hank and Marty stared straight ahead, holding their breath. John watched as the officer conversed with Hal before returning to his car. Hal drove off, blinking his lights to signal John to continue. John started the engine and drove on. Marty and Hank continued in a deep freeze without commenting.

Arriving at the service station, John parked the car and approached the truck. Hal had a grin on his face from ear to ear. "What the fuck was that all about?" John asked.

"Nothing, nothing at all. It was Officer Goody. He stopped me to say he saw the sign at the shop and was sorry to see things did not work out. He wished me luck. That was it."

Marty, Hank, and Hal put their suitcases in the station wagon. John put his luggage in the truck. They dumped the wooden crates behind the service station, secured the vehicles, and went for breakfast.

John chose to have breakfast at the restaurant located on the same block as the bank. He wanted to view the morning bank traffic. Luckily, there was a booth by the window that had a direct view of the bank.

John was shocked to hear Marty and Hank order breakfast consisting of only a bagel and coffee. John stared at the two of them and smiled. John ordered French toast with bacon. Hal only ordered toast and coffee.

John hardly touched his French toast. He ate pieces of bacon, his eyes focused on the bank entrance. The traffic was nonstop. John checked his watch, which read 9:15. No sign of letting up.

"I hope that this is a good sign with all the traffic happening in the morning hours," John said.

"You could bet your mortgage on it, John," Hal replied with confidence.

They finished breakfast by ten. John paid the check and they returned to the shop.

Arriving at the shop, John cruised the area two times to make certain that there were no police in the area before entering the shop. He instructed the guys to put on their rubber gloves again. Since they had used the car that morning, they had to wipe the entire car again. Marty bitched about having to do it again, and, as usual, he lost the argument. He put on the gloves with the others and started wiping the car.

Cleaning finished, John ordered them to straighten out the place. "If we had brooms we could do a much better job," John said, looking around the shop.

"Hell, John there is two brooms and a mop located behind the door of the men's room." Marty was standing next to Hal and kicked him in the shins for opening his mouth. John told Marty and Hank to sweep the floor from wall to wall. Hal would mop the office.

When all the chores were completed, they settled into the office. John took the chair. Hal quickly scampered up the ladder to the loft and retrieved the weapons. He brought them to the office and laid them on the desk. They each took a weapon and inserted the ammunition. John already had his weapon loaded.

After a ten-minute break, John turned to Hal. "You have one more mission to accomplish on the way to the bank: that is to purchase two pairs of nylon stockings that we'll use as masks during the heist." He gave Hal the money.

John checked his watch again. Eleven forty-five. One hour to go.

"Okay, listen up. Since Hal's role of the electrician is out and he's now included in the heist, I'll go over the plan one last time."

"Hank, you will be driving the getaway car. We arrive at the bank at approximately twelve o'clock sharp. You park the car and we wait for Jackson's signal. If it's a go, then Hal, Marty, and I enter the bank. Hank, you remain parked in front of the bank with the motor running. Repeat: keep the motor running. Got that?"

"Gotcha, John," Hank answered.

"Hal, you enter the bank and take the bank guard. Marty you follow Hal, going directly to the bank manager's desk with your gun to his head. You have to move fast, Marty, since there is fifty feet between you and the manager's desk.

"I'll be last in line and go directly to the tellers and cover them. I'll pick up the money from the vault. We can't waste any time. We have to get in and get out within six and a half minutes as planned. If there are any problems with the bank employees or customers, shoot the bastards," John said.

"In the event anything goes wrong, we're to shoot it out. No way will I do any more time in that fuckin' prison." He looked at them. All three hesitated for a second before agreeing. John was satisfied that the issue was settled.

John told Hank that it was time to put on the police uniforms and coveralls. They dressed simultaneously. John was surprised to see Hank's uniform was a perfect fit. John and Hank put the coveralls over the uniforms. John told them to relax for ten minutes.

Later, John looked at his watch. "Okay. Twelve twenty-five. Time." They checked their weapons and tucked them into their waistbands.

John looked around the shop one final time. They put on their latex gloves and got into the car, except Hal. He opened the door slowly and looked up and down the street. It was all clear. He directed Hank to drive out. He then closed the door and made sure that it was unlocked. He jumped into the back seat. Hank drove to find a lingerie shop. John reminded Hal to purchase the most transparent nylons available.

Hal was out of the shop in five minutes. He gave each of them a stocking. They headed for the bank.

There was stillness in the air. It was cool but there was no breeze. John checked his watch: twelve forty-four and no sign of Jackson. John looked for any signs of the law.

He was beginning to get pissed. Twelve forty-five. He directed Hank to drive into the bank parking lot. Hank started the engine and was about to shift gears.

"Hold it, Hank," John yelled. "There he is." As Jackson stepped outside, he lit a cigarette, took two quick puffs, quickly tossed the cigarette to the sidewalk; and went back into the bank.

John checked his watch and the countdown began: ten, nine, eight, seven, six, five, four, three, two, one—"Move . . . . Move"

They put the stockings over their faces, got out of the car, and walked quickly to the bank. With guns tucked against their stomachs, they climbed the steps to the revolving door, with Hal leading the way.

He stepped inside, directly to where the guard was seated on his stool. The guard was caught totally by surprise as Hal pressed the gun to his ribs.

Marty followed, racing across the floor pointing his gun at the manager. He pressed the gun to the manager's head when he reached him.

John followed directly behind Marty to the teller's location and ordered the tellers and two customers to hit the floor and stay put and no one would get hurt. John accessed the vault. The door was open, but the inner gate was closed and locked. He yelled to the manager to release the gate lock. The manager was so stunned that he could not react fast enough. John was looking at Marty, who cocked the hammer of his pistol, when the manager suddenly realized that he was about to be shot. The man released the lock, allowing John access to the vault. At that same time, the manager pressed the silent alarm on the floor below his desk with his left foot.

John emerged from the vault with four canvas bags. He tossed them to the floor toward the exit, and started for the door. Marty immediately followed him, walking backwards while keeping the manager in full view. They picked up the moneybags and went through the revolving door. Hal was the last. He backed out of the bank, down the steps, and then walked briskly to the sidewalk and directly to the car. Hank had the motor racing, then in gear, and they were gone within seconds.

John had misestimated the time of the heist by five seconds, for it had taken six minutes and twenty-five seconds.

In the meantime, Jackson had activated the alarm switch as the manager kept his foot on the button. The police were now responding with sirens screaming.

The people in the bank, being in complete shock, did not move for what seemed to be several minutes. The robbery that could never happen had indeed happened. The guys made a clean getaway but still faced the roadblock.

The manager regained his composure. Upon hearing the police sirens, he rose from his desk and met the police at the bank entrance. He yelled at the first officer who entered that he had delayed in responding to the alarm. The officer was at lost for words. However, the sergeant was close behind and countered, saying the alarm did not sound in his precinct.

"Bullshit!" The manager yelled. "My foot was pressed firmly on the button as soon as I realized it was a robbery. The morning verification with the precincts checked out perfectly," The manager yelled with frustration.

Embarrassed, the sergeant paused and told the manager. "No problem. The roadblocks are in place. Those punks aren't going anywhere."

*   *   *

Arriving at the shop, John directed Hal to count out Jackson's share of the money and store it in the designated area.

"Marty. You drive the getaway car, approximately ten blocks up the street. Park the car and walk one block to the intersection and wait for me."

Marty drove off. John and Hank took off their coveralls and adjusted their uniforms. Hal went to the police car and climbed into the trunk. John got into the police car and pulled out to the driveway. Hank closed the shop door and immediately jumped into the car. John was on his way. He picked up Marty, who climbed into the back seat and laid face down on the floor.

The final phase had begun. John activated the emergency lights and with siren blasting, headed toward State Street and out of town.

Sure enough, they encountered the roadblock a quarter of a mile ahead, with every bit of space taken up by police cars. With fifty yards to go, John saw a police officer waving both arms for him to stop. John slowed down a bit.

At that point, a police sergeant noticed the officer waving John to stop.

"What the hell are you doing? Can't you see that's a police car? Let him through," a sergeant yelled.

The officer backed off; the sergeant then ordered a police car moved to allow John room to get through.

John arrived as one of the cars was moved, giving him just enough clearance to get by. He continued down the road to the abandoned service station.

Hank could not believe that they had actually pulled it off. Arriving at the service station, they parked the police car behind the building. John unlocked the trunk. Hal got out laughing and shook John's hand.

"Okay. Put the moneybags in the truck. I'll drive the truck. You guys will ride in the station wagon to the shopping center. We'll transfer the money into the station wagon, ditch the truck somewhere in the shopping center, and we're home free."

Marty stared at John, "Why put the money in the truck? Why not put the money in the station wagon and ditch the truck here and now?" Marty asked.

John glared back at Marty as Hank and Hal, with mouths wide open, wondered what to expect next.

"You know, Marty, you picked a fine time to question my integrity, but I'll answer you anyway. If the police noticed four men in a car and proceeded to stop them and decided to search the car and find the money, we're dead.

Would you stop a business truck with one person to ask if he had just robbed, a bank?"

Marty studied John for a second. "You're right, but let Hal or Hank drive the truck. You drive the station wagon. You know this area. You've been this way before."

John handed the keys to Marty. "Okay Marty. You drive the truck."

Marty told John that he did not want to drive the truck. He recommended Hal or Hank drive. John said fine and took the keys from Marty and handed them to Hank. He didn't want to drive the truck either, so.

Marty looked at Hal who also declined to drive the truck.

John turned to Marty. "Well, Marty. Time is wasting. Every minute we lose, the police gain three minutes on us." Marty stared at all three and finally agreed that John should drive the truck. He gave John the key, and John in turn handed it to Hank.

John told them he would follow close behind and meet up with them at the shopping center. He also told Hank not to spare the gas. They jumped in the vehicles and were off.

Hank followed John's instructions. He was doing eighty to ninety miles an hour with John maintaining a safe distance behind.

Hank came to a downgrade, where the road was winding with a deep ravine to the left. He decided he had better slow down. He applied his foot to the brake and got no response. He glanced at the brake pedal to make certain his foot was in the correct position. He applied the brakes again and started pumping for all he was worth.

"What the fuck? What the fuck?" Hank started yelling at the top of his lungs.

"What's the hell is wrong?" Marty asked.

"No fucking brakes!!" As the car progressively picked up speed exceeding over a hundred miles an hour, Hank had his hands full negotiating the curves on the winding road. With no sign of the road leveling off, and a ravine to his left, the momentum became deadly.

He tried scraping the dirt embankment on the right side of the road as a brake. Marty suddenly realized what had happened, and cried, "John! Fucking John double-crossed us, the greedy bastard." Hank lost the battle with the car as he bounced off the embankment and veered to the left, catapulting over the ravine.

"John, you mother fuckerrrrrrrrrrrrrrr," Marty screamed on the way down.

The crash was fierce, a raging ball of fire. No one could possibly survive the inferno.

John parked the truck. He emptied all but half of the last bag on the floor of the truck. With the canvas bags, he ran down the ravine to the crash sight. He managed to get close enough to the burning car to scatter the money, and toss the bags into the blaze. He turned and ran back to the truck, watching as the fire continued to burn.

Suddenly, John felt remorse for Hank because he had liked Hank and would have spared him. However, Hank was caught up in a numbers game. Without a third body the case would remain open.

The gas tank finally blew. Thick black smoke blanketed the area. John was now the sole owner of all the money, and he decided he'd better get the hell out of there before someone noticed the smoke.

Sabotaging the brakes while retrieving his lost wallet had worked—Marty was right to be suspicious of John.

*   *   *

The bank had closed early for the police investigation. After preliminary questioning, the bank employees were allowed to leave so that the bank could be searched for clues.

Jackson left the bank and walked briskly to the parking lot. He got into his car and drove quickly to the shop. Arriving, he opened the door and drove his car into the shop. He rushed to the ladder leading to the loft and climbed up. His anxiety to reach the money caused him to lose his balance, and he went crashing to the shop floor. He clutched his knee for a second, but immediately bounced up thinking about the money; he felt no pain. He scampered back up the ladder and finally reached the designated area where he found the carton. Upon seeing the cash, he sighed with relief. He fell to his knees, scooped up the money with both hands and tossed it into the air. He lifted the box to catch the bills as they drifted downward. Happy and satisfied, he picked up the carton and scampered back down the ladder.

He placed the box in the trunk of the car and backed out of the garage.

He took the garage key and locked the door.

*   *   *

Jackson decided to return the key to the realtor immediately rather than wait until evening only if no one was in the office. Upon arriving he parked the car, a block away and walked slowly by the office looking through the window. No one was in the office, and the door was locked. He looked up and down the street to make certain that no one was watching, he leaned forward and dropped the key in the mail slot. He turned around and walked briskly back to his car. He drove off with all his problems behind him.

*   *   *

John arrived at the shopping mall and went directly to the Sears store to purchase two large suitcases to store the money. As he was leaving the store, he passed through the television department to see every television on display showing the story of the robbery. In fact, it made the national news as well. John asked a watching bystander what had happened.

"A perfect bank robbery, and the stupid jerks screwed it up by getting themselves killed. Shame. A perfect job and clean getaway," the guy said.

John thanked him and left the store triumphant. Arriving at the truck, he placed the money in the two suitcases, which barely contained all the bills. He drove to Chicago a very rich man.

Arriving in Chicago at seven-thirty the following morning, John stopped at a diner. There he purchased a sweet bun and coffee-to-go, as well as a local newspaper, and then drove to his apartment.

Parking the truck in the apartment lot, he took the suitcases and hurried up to his room. Placing the suitcases on the bed, he immediately opened the first one to reveal a bright flash of green that seemed to put him in a trance. He could not take his gaze from the money as he opened the second suitcase. He looked for a secure hiding place for the loot. He recalled that there was a crawl space located in the ceiling of his bedroom closet. He stood on a chair and removed the trap door. He stacked the money neatly in and around the crawl space. Money secured, he replaced the trap door and stacked shoeboxes, hiding the access.

With the loot taken care of, he kicked off his shoes, removed his shirt, and made himself comfortable. He sat on his easy chair, took a mouth full of coffee, which was already lukewarm, and picked up the newspaper. He could not miss the headlines printed in four inch letters: "SUCCESSFUL BANK ROBBERY IN WORTHINGTON, OHIO, NEGATED BY FIERY CRASH.'

John read the fine print and found what he was hoping to see: "No survivors and the bodies were burned beyond recognition."

Suddenly John's eyes focused on a question posed by the newspaper editor: "Is it possible that the thieves may have had inside help?" That query struck John like a bolt of lightning, so roughly that he abruptly realized he had one final mission to accomplish in order to complete the cycle. He must eliminate that final possible threat: Mr. Jackson. John feared that the editor's note would influence the police to begin an investigation of bank personnel. John began thinking madly. Jackson, with all that money, would most likely start spending well above his means. John recalled that Jackson drank excessively at their two meetings. Too much drinking would eventually lead to intoxication and excessive talk, creating suspicion. All this would eventually lead to John. He immediately formulated his strategy: he would fly to Worthington and take a limo to a motel within walking distance of restaurants and clubs. He would contact Jackson for a friendly dinner and a drink or two . . .

*   *   *

Tears streamed down both cheeks as Kay stared at the paper reporting the news of the robbery and the fiery crash and the demise of the thieves.

"He was telling the truth all along, saying that he was in town to rob the bank."

Suddenly she realized that the paper only listed three bodies. She knew there were four in John's group. She thought and hoped that it was John who survived the crash. She also hoped that if he indeed survived, he would return and look her up. She dressed for work.

*   *   *

Pat Reardon, the special agent for the Federal Bureau of Investigation in charge of investigating the Worthington bank caper, was in the bank interviewing the bank manager, Mr. Roger Brown. He began by asking Brown about engaging the alarm system.

"As I said earlier, I activated the alarm as soon as I realized there was a robbery," Brown answered, obviously upset. He further informed agent Reardon that as far as he could make out, there were only three individuals involved in the robbery.

"Is it possible that you did not apply enough pressure to the alarm button?" Pat asked.

Perturbed, the manager reminded Pat that the system was tested each and every morning before the bank opened. "Yesterday was no different. The police confirmed the alarm was working."

Pat again turned his attention to the getaway car. "Is it possible that there was a driver waiting in a getaway car, meaning there could have been four rather then three thieves who committed the robbery?"

"By the time I got to the door, the thieves were already gone," Brown answered.

Persistent, Pat asked Brown, "How many minutes would you estimate it took for him to get to the front entrance and look toward the sidewalk?"

By this time Brown was thoroughly angry.

"Look, whatever your name is, with all the excitement, who would think to keep one's mind on the exact time? I did not see how they got away or what method they used. They could have used bicycles for all I know. Excuse me, I am very busy." He turned, walked by Pat and back to his desk. Surprised, Pat took off his hat, scratched his head, and left the bank, heading for the police station.

*   *   *

Chief Daniels was in his office, conducting a staff meeting with his district commanders. He greeted Agent Reardon and introduced him to his commanders, offering him a cup of coffee.

"That's the best offer I had all day, Chief," Pat said.

He sat by Daniels' desk, rolling his coffee cup between his hands; he took a sip, and then placed the cup on the desk. He looked around the table at each commander individually. It was so quiet, you could hear a pin drop.

Daniels looked at Reardon. "Well, Mr. Reardon. You will find out sooner or later if you don't already have an idea. The thieves got through the roadblock using a vehicle made up to look like one of our own. It was so perfect, it fooled everyone."

Reardon looked at the chief. "You mean, lights, sirens, the works?"

"The whole nine yards," Daniels answered.

Reardon now realized the cars were switched outside of town. He asked if they had recovered the fake police car.

"No, but we're still searching. When we locate it, I'll let you know."

Daniels went on to admit that the robbery was expertly planned and executed. He concluded the meeting, and the commanders left the room with the exception of Reardon, who remained.

Pat consoled Chief Daniels by telling him that things like this happen now and again. "One consolation is, they did not get away with it."

Reardon placed his coffee cup on the desk. He took the photographs of the destroyed station wagon, strewn on the chief's desk. He studied each one thoroughly. Pat just shook his head.

"Something wrong?" Daniels asked.

"I cannot believe that the robbery was pulled off by only three punks. There had to be a fourth person. The fourth person being the driver."

Daniels reminded him that there were no eyewitnesses to verify a fourth person, if there was a fourth person.

Pat agreed, studied the photographs again, and asked, "Were there any positive identifications of the bodies?"

"None whatsoever. Too badly burned. Even the state license plate could not be identified. We will, however, try dental records tomorrow, but I have no confidence that would work."

"Oh! One of the suitcases found at the crash sight was not totally destroyed by the fire."

"And?" Questioned Pat.

"Nothing, nothing except for some clothing and a pair of shoes. One shirt had the initials M.S. You know what that means."

"You got it chief. There are a million people with the same initials. How about the money?" Pat asked.

"Also completely burned with the exception of a few bills scattered in and around the crash site."

"Well, I guess there's not much more we can do except . . ."

"Except what?" Asked the chief.

"Something that the bank manager mentioned. He was emphatic about holding his foot firmly on the silent alarm button while the robbery was in progress. Yet nothing sounded in the precincts."

"You mean . . . ?"

"Precisely. The thieves may have had inside help. Someone could have deactivated then activated the alarm system before and after the robbery."

"Good thinking, Mr. Reardon. I'll have two of my men investigate that possibility immediately."

"Good idea. If you come up with a possible lead be sure and contact me."

"Will do," Said the chief.

Pat took a sip of coffee. "Well, I guess this case is closed. My job is finished unless something turns up. I'll check out of my hotel and leave for Cleveland in the morning." He thanked Chief Daniels for his help and left.

*　　*　　*

The plane touched down at 9:15 a.m. and the limo ride to Worthington took all of one hour and twenty minutes. After registering at a motel in town, John decided to relax for an hour or so.

He was lying on the bed, and of all things was browsing through the Bible that he had picked up from the end table. He glanced at the clock-radio on the night table reflecting the time for lunch. He dressed casually: shorts, a pullover shirt, and a pair of white sneakers. He left his motel room and walked to a nearby restaurant. After lunch, he went to a phone, checked the bank's phone number, and dialed. It was no surprise to John to find that Mr. Jackson had taken the day off. John was beginning to feel uncomfortable. At six he took a shower and went to have supper and a drink or two. The restaurant was unusually crowded. Then John realized that it was happy hour. He sat at the bar and joined the crowd, who seemed to be having a blast. In fact, there were more girls than men. But to John's surprise, the town folks had recovered quickly from the shock of the bank robbery. Now that he thought about it, the Worthington Review from the airport did not have one article referring to it. Even conversations that he overheard did not include the robbery. Of course, John was not upset about it.

A few girls showed interest in John. He thought about making out, but thought better of it and decided to play it low key. The less he was seen and heard, the better. He nursed three drinks and listened to the music until eight o'clock. He had dinner and returned to the motel. He changed down to his shorts, turned on the television, and watched a baseball game, between the Cleveland Indians and the New York Yankees. As usual, John fell asleep during the game and slept through the playing of the National anthem, ending the day's television programming. Nine o'clock the next morning he left the motel for breakfast, finishing by ten. He looked for and found a coin phone and called the bank. He asked for Jackson. He was relieved to find him at work. Jackson seemed cordial when he heard that it was John, and after a five-minute talk, John asked him if he would like to have dinner and a drink or two after work. Jackson hesitated for a moment, and then accepted John's invitation. John asked him if he would pick him up at the intersection a block from the motel, to which Jackson also agreed. John returned to his motel to evaluate his strategy. He lay on the bed looking at the ceiling. Now his plan was etched in his mind. Step one was to make certain that Jackson got bombed. Step two was to break his neck while in his car. Step three: crash Jackson's vehicle with Jackson inside at the same location where the guys crashed earlier. But John had to make certain that it looked like an accident.

He was not surprised to see Jackson in a new car and sharply dressed. John looked around inside and commented that the car was nice and said that Jackson looked great.

"Thanks to you, Mr. Reed." Jackson smiled. From the looks of things, John did not have to ask Jackson if he were being discreet with his funds. "Where to?" Jackson asked. John mentioned the café going toward the airport. Jackson was familiar with the place, saying it was a little ways out from town.

John answered, "The food is the best I have ever tasted." Jackson agreed and headed out of town toward the restaurant. Lady luck was on John's side again, for the place was crowded. In fact, they had to wait for twenty minutes to be seated, which suited John just fine. They stood by the bar, and Jackson began belting drinks down at a fairly fast pace. They were finally seated and ordered steaks with all the trimmings. During the meal, John kept feeding Jackson drink after drink. As fast as Jackson finished one drink, John ordered a refill. John casually asked Jackson if he had a safe hiding place for his money. "You bet I do, Mr. Reed. In fact, I have it stashed in a safe deposit box," Jackson said with a grin.

"You mean—?"

"No, not my bank, Mr. Reed. There's a bank at the shopping center out of town going toward the airport." Jackson continued grinning. John, relieved, remembered the shopping center. He told Jackson that it was a smart move. Jackson went on to explain to John that he had leased the box for two years. He was now speaking with a slur.

"Is your wife on the card?"

"No, sir. I'm the only one listed on the card. The less the bitch knows the better."

John, really feeling good at this juncture, mentioned the girl that had played him. "Oh, her? No, she got hers. Some guy really beat the shit out of her, and she left town." The stage was set.

The meal finished, Jackson could just about stand up. John paid the tab and they left. With the place crowded, no one seemed to notice Jackson staggering toward the exit with John's help. John volunteered to drive, and Jackson was in no shape to argue. So he handed John the keys, and John drove to the abandoned service station where he'd finish Jackson off. John parked the car behind the service station. He glanced at Jackson and saw that he was in a deep sleep. John climbed in the back seat and leaned forward behind Jackson. He put both arms around his neck and with a quick snap broke it. John got back into the driver's seat and found the bank deposit box key; he put it in his pocket, then drove to the launch site. He arrived at the starting point of the ravine. He turned off the engine and got out of the car to double check the location. Satisfied, he got back into the car and was about to start the engine when suddenly Jackson, who was supposedly dead, became very much alive. Jackson yelled as he attacked John. They wrestled back and forth, John cursing himself for screwing up. Jackson held John tightly by the throat. John began losing his breath. He managed to get one arm free, took a deep gulp, and pushed himself backwards, causing Jackson to hit his head against the ceiling light, temporarily stunning him. This time John gripped Jackson's throat with both arms. He did not let go until he was certain that Jackson was dead. He leaned back on the seat to catch his breath. Then he started the engine, put it in gear, and positioned the car toward the edge of the ravine. He then put the gear in neutral and got out of the car. He pulled Jackson to the driver's side, turned on the headlights, and rolled the window down just enough to get his hand through the window. He leaned in the window, engaged the gear into drive, and the car immediately lurched forward and over the ravine. It seemed to float upwards at first, and then it dived toward the bottom of the ravine, and ended in a fiery crash. John returned to his motel and retired for the night. He awoke early the next morning. He hurried to the motel lobby and purchased a Worthington newspaper hoping to read about an accident. John got his wish. The article on the inner page read: "LOCAL MAN KILLED ON HIGHWAY 61." He was identified as Mr. George Jackson of Worthington. The coroner's report read: Accident was due to driving under the influence. John was elated over the coroner's report. He tossed the paper and went for lunch.

*   *   *

Kay arrived at the diner and was about to enter the ladies room when she noticed someone familiar sitting at the counter. She stood frozen. She slowly moved toward the figure sitting at the counter.

"Are you just going to stand there like a statue, or are you going to say hello?" John said without turning his head.

Realizing that it was John, she placed her hand to her mouth and a tear trickled down her cheek. She walked behind the counter and confronted him. "Hi," she said with a huge smile and dabbing her eyes.

John just stared into her eyes. Should I change seats?"

"No. You're just fine. I'm working the counter today." as she waved to the waitress she was relieving. John gave her a five dollar's and told her to give it to the other waitress. Fortunately there was only a few customers in the diner. John and Kay could converse as long as they wished. She took the coffee pot from the burner and refilled his cup. She noticed that he had not eaten; at least there wasn't a plate in front of him. "Something to eat?" She asked.

"No thanks, just coffee would be fine.

Kay was smart enough not to ask what he was doing at the diner and did not dare mention the bank robbery. In the meantime two customers sat at the counter. Kay immediately furnished them with utensils, water and a menu.

John continued drinking his coffee. After serving the two customers Kay returned to John. "So?" Kay stared into his eyes. "So what? John answered.

I'm here to spend a day a two with you, that's if you can afford to take two days off." John stared back at her.

"Two days! She answered back. I'd take a year off if you asked me to."

"I bet you would at that." John continued. He furnished her the name of his motel and room number. "How about meeting me there after getting off from work and . . . ."

"I'll notify my boss and meet you there," gleamed Kay.

"Great." Oh, I'll need a ride to the airport afterwards."

"No problem." She answered.

*   *   *

John was lying on the bed browsing through the local newspaper when he was jolted by a loud knock at his door. He slowly opened the door to Kay standing before him dressed in the sexiest outfit he had seen. She looked spectacular! They immediately fell into each other arms. For the next two days, they never left the room except to grab a bite to eat.

When John was ready to leave town, Kay drove him to the airport. She wished they were able to spend more time together.

When they arrived at the airport, John got out of the car and walked around to the driver's side to give Kay one last kiss. As she rolled up the window she smiled and swooned, "Thanks for a lovely two days."

"The pleasure was all mine." He smiled.

Kay watched him until he disappeared into the crowd. Just as she started the car she noticed a package on the passenger seat. She stared at it for a moment then ripped it open, shocked at the sight before her. It was more money then she ever had in her possession at one time. A tear trickled down her cheek. She started the car and was on her way home.

*   *   *

John wore a smile the entire flight to Chicago. Arriving home early that afternoon, he showered and took a nap.

John woke up to darkness. He had slept the afternoon into the evening. He was hungry and ready for supper. He washed, shaved, walked to the closet, and looked up to check out the money's location, which was now becoming an obsession for him. He got into the truck, not sure where to have supper. He drove around and happened to pass the deli where Sid worked and thought that it would be a good idea to show up and have Sid see him alive and well. This would prevent John's name from being tossed around and possibly connecting him with the Worthington robbery. He entered the deli and found Sid sitting at the cash register. "Hi Sid. How about one of your specials? I'm so hungry I could eat a bear." John smiled.

Sid was so shocked upon seeing John that he lost his breath as if he were having a heart attack. Finally, he got up from the chair. "John, you son-of-a-bitch. I thought you was one of . . . . you know?"

John asked for the house special, then said he would explain afterwards.

Sid yelled, "The special," to the old guy behind the counter. "So. So. Tell me!"

John explained that he chickened out and begged the others to change their minds, but they would not hear of it. John really laid it on as Sid stared at him wide-eyed.

"Yes, but they did. They got away with it then fucked themselves. Do you know if they used my suggestion for the alarm system?"

"Apparently they did, Sid, and it worked," John said. He went on to explain that he thought it would not work because the bank would probably check with the utility company and the police.

Sid agreed. He paused, as a customer approached to pay for a takeout.

"Oy vay! All that money went up in smoke! What a waste . . . . what a waste."

Sid asked John how well he knew "the three who, you know . . ."

"As far as I know, Sid, they were from Cleveland, and I met them while in prison." He did not want him to know about Hank. It could complicate things.

"At least you're alive and not with your friends," Sid said.

In the meantime, a deli worker brought John a platter of hot roast beef, potato salad with a pickle, and a cold beer. John dug in. He drank another beer with Sid. "I have to get going, Sid. I have to pay a few bills," John lied. Sid stood up and embraced John. About to leave, John reached for his billfold. He took out two twenties.

"This is for the check, and the balance is your tip." Sid accepted the money. John left and returned to his apartment. After entering, he walked directly to the bedroom and the closet to check the money's location. Afterward, he undressed down to his shorts, turned on the television, and dozed off. He awoke to a blank television screen. He turned off the television and turned in for the night.

*   *   *

The next morning in Worthington, Pat was at the hotel desk checking out when the desk phone rang. It was answered by the clerk, "Yes, he's here about to check out of the hotel. Yes sir, one moment please." He handed Reardon the phone. "Chief Daniels, Mr. Reardon."

"Hi chief, what's up?"

"Good morning Mr. Reardon. I just called to inform you that I believe that we found the get-a-way car. It was discovered approximately five blocks from the bank.

"Thanks Chief," Pat said. "I'll meet you at your office post haste. Have the coffee ready." He told the clerk to hold his room until further notice.

Pat sat with his feet propped up on Daniels' desk clutching a coffee cup with both hands. "Where's the car now chief?"

"It was towed to the station back lot." He further informed Chief Daniels that Officer Harris, while having supper at Ben's the other evening, had witnessed an individual getting personal with Kay Williams, a waitress.

Pat recommended that they speak to Officer Harris first and then inspect the car. Chief Daniels directed Sergeant Tate to send in Officer Harris.

Officer Harris was somber and nervously turned his hat in a circular motion with both hands.

Daniels tried to make him feel comfortable, telling him to relax and be seated.

"How long have you been a policeman, Officer Harris?" he asked.

"Two years and two months, sir," Harris stuttered.

"Fine. Now, explain to me and Mr. Reardon what you observed while having supper at Ben's."

"Well sir, Kay the waitress was taking orders from two men sitting at her table, when suddenly she slapped one of them. I didn't know the reason why she did so. However, I suspected that one of them was probably getting fresh with her." He paused, still rolling his hat between his hands.

"And?" Chief Daniels asked.

"Well, sir, after hearing the disturbance and noticing what happened, I approached the individual to arrest him for disorderly conduct, but she, I mean, Kay, paused as she stared at one of the two then told me it was all right, she had everything under control. So I went back to my dinner."

Pat turned to Harris and asked, "Why would you believe that this event was strange?"

"Well, sir. For some reason they didn't appear to be local folks, and the way Kay looked at the other fellow . . . ."

Pat looked intensely at the officer. "Officer Harris, the two men who were sitting at the table, could you possibly describe them and give me their approximate height?"

"I think so, sir. They were both Caucasian. One fella was approximately five foot-five, the other one about five-foot, seven," Harris answered.

"Do you think that you could identify the two men through mug shots?" Pat asked.

"It would be kinda tough, sir," Harris answered, "with the lights turned down and everything happening so fast."

"Anymore questions, Mr. Reardon?"

Pat looked at Officer Harris, "Are you certain that there were only two men sitting at the table and not three or possibly four? Or was it possible that one or two persons may have gone to the rest room?"

"Well sir, with all the confusion, I could have missed maybe one more person but not a fourth."

Pat signaled Chief Daniels, who then excused Officer Harris. Daniels looked at Pat. "What do you think?"

Pat asked to see the photographs of the bodies again, which he studied for several minutes. Then he told Daniels that the descriptions of the men at the restaurant and the bodies of the robbers were one and the same.

"Well, I guess the bank manager was correct, saying there were only three men involved in the hold-up."

Pat answered, "Let's see what information the car has to offer, and then visit the waitress. Maybe she could shed some light on the case."

*   *   *

At three o'clock in the morning, John awoke to a nightmare of Marty, Hank, and Hal standing over him.

"Why did you murder us, John?" they asked.

John screamed "NOOOO!"

He quickly sat up and turned on the light. His body was covered with perspiration, and he leaned back on the bed to catch his breath. He took a towel and wiped his body. He went to the fridge, found a bottle of cold wine, and poured himself a glass.

He could hardly hold the wine glass to his lips, his hands were trembling so.

In fact, he had to grasp the glass with both hands. He finished the wine and went back to bed.

He leaned back and said to himself, *What the fuck is wrong with you, John? Going soft all of a sudden? The man without a conscious. Straighten up, guy, or you'll end up on a funny farm.* Finally relaxed, he turned over and went back to sleep, for all of three hours. He awoke at six and realized that he was up for the day.

He went to the bathroom and showered before leaving to have breakfast at a dinner where he was known.

When he walked in, the waitresses converged on John and greeted him. Lori Smith, a long-time waitress, was a thirty-five year-old bleached blond. Her hair fluffed high, stiff with hair spray. She had a well proportioned body. Since she knew John and dated him on occasion, she was the first to speak.

"Hi, stranger, I haven't seen you for quite sometime. Did you find a better place to eat?" Lori asked.

"You know I wouldn't desert you, Lori," John answered with a smile.

"My mother has been ill, and I had to take care of her. Thank the Lord; she's feeling much better now. I'm taking her on a vacation, and you may not see me for a while." John was laying the groundwork for his trip to the Bahamas, so that he won't be missed again.

All the waitresses, especially Lori, thought it was nice of him to look after his mother's welfare.

John sat in a booth and ordered steak and eggs over easy, home fries, wheat toast, and coffee—black. When he finished breakfast, he waved for Lori and asked her, "Are you up to a night out on the town and love-making?"

"I'm always up to making love with you, John. You know that," she purred.

"It's a date," John said. "I'll pick you up tonight at nine." He picked up the check and placed a ten-dollar tip on the table. "See you at nine." He left the diner for his monthly visit with his parole officer, Mr. Sherman.

*   *   *

John entered the parole office and was greeted by the receptionist, Mrs. Winters. She was in her middle fifties. She was short, thin, and well-put-together for a woman her age, a brunette with a gray streak on one side of fluffed-up hair. She was dressed conservatively, with a black spring skirt below her knees and a white silk blouse that showed her bra. She was quite fond of John.

"Mr. John Reed, reporting to his parole officer," John said with a huge smile.

"Hi, Mr. Reed. You look chipper today." She smiled.

"I'm feeling the way I look because of you, Mrs. Winters," John said.

"Oh, go on with you, Mr. Reed!" She blushed. "I'll tell Mr. Sherman you're here."

John thanked her, picked an easy chair, sat, and watched her as she disappeared into Mr. Sherman's office.

"Mr. Sherman will see you now, Mr. Reed."

John thanked her again. "It's a shame that your married Mr. Winters."

John's remark caused her to blush again.

Mr. Sherman was a college dropout, in his mid-forties, tall and muscular, his broad shoulders wider than the chair he was sitting in. His dark brown hair was cut close to his skull, military style.

He was dressed in beaten Levis and a denim jacket over a blue cotton shirt. For a civil service employee of Chicago, one would think that a coat and tie would be appropriate.

He greeted John with a handshake.

"Have a seat, John. So, how is the world treating you, and are you staying out trouble?"

"Straight as an arrow, Mr. Sherman. There's no way that I'm going back to that dungeon, and I'm doing fine," John said.

"Good for you, Mr. Reed." Sherman smiled. He paused for a second or so and shuffled a few papers in John's folder. He looked up at John and asked him what he thought about the big bank robbery in Ohio.

John looked at him. Coolly, calmly, and collectedly he said, "What robbery? I don't recall reading or seeing anything on television about a bank robbery. I heard some people mentioning a big crash at the diner the other day. Tell you the truth, Mr. Sherman, I'm a sports freak. I mostly read and watch sports. I read the business report on occasions. That's about it."

Mr. Sherman went on to explain the robbery in detail to John.

"Wow. A perfect crime and the idiots screwed it up. Like you always said, Mr. Sherman, crime does not pay." John assumed that Sherman was testing his reaction to the news.

"That's fine, John. Now, what can I do for you?"

"As a matter of fact, sir, I would like to take a vacation in the Bahamas. Possibly get a job and reside there for an indefinite period . . ."

Sherman opened John's file again and glanced through it.

"Well, since you only have six months left on your parole, something could be worked out. However, I would have to check with my superiors of the board. In fact, I'm scheduled to meet with them at three this afternoon. If the board approves your request, you would only be required to call the office at the end of each month. I'll put a plug in for you John."

The only plug he put in for anything was his toaster. *The prick,* John thought to himself.

"Tell you what. Call me in the morning. I should have an answer for you then. Oh, by the way, I'll need an address where you'll be staying."

John had no idea where he would be staying but agreed and left Mr. Sherman's office.

On the way out he blew a kiss to Mrs. Winters. "By the way, if you ever divorce your husband, let me know," John kidded.

"Oh, Mr. Reed," she giggled.

*　　*　　*

Back in Worthington, Pat and Chief Daniels walked to the rear of the police parking lot. They arrived to find the lab people examining the car for fingerprints.

Pat asked the lab technician for a pair of rubber gloves and began searching inside the car.

"Not one print, sir." The lab technician shook his head. "It's very strange that there were no fingerprints at all."

Pat looked at the lab technician. "It's not strange at all. There are no signs of fingerprints because this vehicle was used as the getaway car in the robbery of the Worthington bank." Pat grinned.

Chief Daniels was surprised and asked how he knew.

Pat explained, "If anyone used this car every day or even once a week, you would find his or her fingerprints somewhere—the door handle, steering wheel—somewhere. It's apparent the thieves wiped the entire car clean and used gloves during the clean-up. My guess is that the robbers used latex gloves."

The lab technician and Chief Daniels looked at each other and then back at Pat with amazement.

"Good thinking, Mr. Reardon," said Daniels. The lab technician just shook his head.

Pat looked at Chief Daniels, and both decided to call it a day.

"How about we visit the waitress's apartment in the morning?" Pat asked Daniels.

"Fine, let's do it."

"Oh, one more thing, chief. Have the coffee ready," Pat said, laughing.

*　　*　　*

At six in the morning, Lori awakened John. He leaned over, checked the clock, and could not believe that she was up so early, since they were up the entire evening dining, dancing, and making love until dawn. John calculated that she had secured a total of three hours of sleep.

He lay back in bed and waited until she showered.

Lori made the mistake of only wearing a towel when she returned. The second mistake was to sit by his side.

"What the hell are you doing up so early?"

"I'm a working girl, you know, and must be in work by nine."

"You mean you could work this day with only three hours sleep?"

She reminded him that she was still young.

"Are you trying to tell me that I'm an old man?"

"If the shoe fits . . ." she said. Without warning, he attacked her, ripped off the towel, and positioned her for sex. She pleaded saying that she had to be in work by nine.

Their sex act ended, he bounced from the bed to the bathroom with Lori close behind to cleanup.

John showered while she dressed and put on her face. She offered to buy him breakfast, which he accepted. She used her car while he took the truck.

The diner was in full swing. He took a newspaper from a vending machine and sat at the first booth by the door. He shuffled through the newspaper for any news about the heist.

In the meantime, Lori brought him a large glass of orange juice and followed it with steak and eggs. His gaze focused on her backside and he whistled. She kept walking and turned her head, giving him a sexy smile.

He just sat there shaking his head. He finished his breakfast, placed a twenty-dollar bill on the table, and left.

Arriving at his apartment, John opened the door to what appeared to be advertising flyers scattered on the floor. Pissed, he picked them up and threw them in the trash container. Then, as though drawn by a magnet, he walked directly to the bedroom closet and looked up at the trap door. He suddenly realized that this practice of always checking out the money's location was becoming an obsession.

I'd better get a hold of myself or I'll end up a loony tune, he told himself. Since he was already at the closet, he replenished his billfold with extra cash. He went to the living room and sat in his armchair, read the paper, and listened to his favorite opera before dozing off. He awoke in time to call Mother Hubbard for his verdict regarding his trip to the Bahamas.

He was prepared to joke with the receptionist, but Mr. Sherman answered the phone. After the greeting, Mr. Sherman told him to come to his office.

John told him he was on his way and prepared himself for the worst. He looked around for the receptionist when he arrived. Mr. Sherman noticed and informed him that this was her day off. He told John to have a seat. "I have good news, and I have bad news."

Again John thought the worst. Mr. Sherman continued, "The good news is that you can go to the Islands and stay indefinitely. The bad news is, you have to report in person each month until the termination of your parole."

John told him he could live with that. John further told Mr. Sherman that he would furnish him the address immediately upon arriving.

John shook his hand and thanked him.

Mr. Sherman wished him luck. John thanked him again and left.

*   *   *

On his way home the sign "Elaine's Travel Agency" caught his eye. He entered the agency. There she sat: a living blond-haired, blue-eyed beauty wearing a blue, tight outfit with a low neck line that revealed the tops of her breasts. She sat with her legs crossed, and the dress, being well-above her knees, exposed her thighs.

Her beauty awed John. Hank always said if John fell in shit, he'd come out smelling like a rose. This was no exception.

"Can I help you?" she asked in a pleasing voice.

"Yes, thank you. I would like to speak with Elaine," John stared into her eyes.

"I'm Elaine. How can I help you?" she smiled.

"I'm planning on taking a vacation to the Bahamas," John said.

"Great! This is your lucky day," she replied.

"You could say that again," his eyes focused on her legs.

"I'm sorry?" She said looking into his eyes.

"No. Nothing. I was just thinking out loud."

She asked him to have a seat and described a special on a cruise beginning Saturday, sailing from New York to the Bahamas for only five hundred and fifty dollars.

"The package includes round trip airfare to New York and meals. If you're flexible, it's a great deal," she said.

"I'm very flexible and can leave on a minute's notice if required. However, I have a few questions to ask you," John said smiling.

"Fire away, Mr . . . . ?"

"Reed. John Reed," he answered. "What if I decided to stay an extra week or so?"

"No. I'm sorry. You must return as scheduled or forfeit your return trip and you would have to finance your own return." Apologizing, she explained it was company policy.

"No need to apologize. I understand," John answered.

She changed body positions, exposing more of her thighs.

John was upset because the way he was seated prevented him from taking full advantage of the view.

She reiterated that it was a special price and probably would not be repeated for quite sometime. She looked directly into his eyes. John did all he could to keep from jumping over the desk and kissing her.

"Funny," she said, "I happen to be going on the same cruise."

John's eyes lit up like a Christmas tree. "You don't say?"

"Yes," she nodded.

"Vacation?" he asked.

"No. Compliments of the tour company."

She explained that the various resorts offer free sample vacations to travel agencies. "They're called promotions. It gives the travel agency the opportunity to see vacation resorts for themselves, which makes it easy for the travel agent to sell the customer."

John wasn't really interested hearing a complete explanation, but he had asked for it. He had heard enough when she said she was going on the same cruise.

"If you'll have dinner with me on the cruise, I'll sign on the dotted line this very minute," John said.

"You mean you're going solo? I mean alone? No wife or girlfriend?" she asked.

"Just little ol' me." He laughed.

She smiled and took the forms from her desk and began filling them out with the information furnished by John. She asked him, "Cash or charge?"

"Cash," he answered. "Hold on. Do we have a dinner date?"

"Of course."

"Oh. One more question if I may," John said.

"Fire away," she answered.

"To what island are we sailing?"

"Oh, I'm sorry," she said, "I should have explained the itinerary. We fly from Chicago to New York. We sail from New York to the Island of Nassau and return. There is a one-day layover before returning. You have the option of visiting the other islands like Freeport and other small islands."

With no further questions, John handed her five one hundred dollars bills. She thanked him and told him that she would have his airline and cruise tickets Friday or early Saturday morning.

"If you don't mind, I'd rather pick up the tickets Saturday morning at the airport."

"No problem." She thanked him again and told him that she would see him at O'Hare Airport on Saturday morning at eight.

John decided to invite her to dinner that evening.

"I'm sorry, I already have plans for this evening."

"Okay, how about tomorrow night?"

"I'm sorry, Mr. Reed. I'm booked the entire week."

John wasn't surprised. A beauty like her should have a date practically every night of the week. He asked her if she were engaged or going steady.

"Neither," she answered. "I enjoy being single at the present time with no obligations. If and when Mr. Right comes along, I'll settle down." She saw disappointment in his eyes for the second time.

"Tell you what, Mr. Reed, how about if you and I leave for the airport from my office Saturday morning? We'll share the cab fare. Say sevenish."

John agreed without the slightest hesitation. "One final question if I may."

"Okay," she said.

"Would you by chance know of a reasonably nice hotel in Nassau, if I decide to stay a few additional weeks?"

"No problem. In fact, I'll be staying at the Queen Ann Hotel the day before sailing back to New York. I opted to spend the last night at a hotel rather than the cruise ship. I'll call now if you wish and reserve a room for you. However, I remind you again, if and when you return to New York, it's at your expense."

"No problem," John answered. Elaine picked up the phone, called the hotel, and made the necessary arrangements, charging it to her account. He was set. He took out his billfold again and asked the cost.

"Oh, you can pay me later."

He insisted, so she told him, "Fifty dollars a day, two weeks seven hundred dollars."

He gave her eight one hundred dollar bills and told her the extra hundred was for taxes. "See you Saturday morning at seven."

He put his phone number on a slip of paper and handed it to her. "In the event your plans are canceled for any reason, I'll be ready and waiting in the wings."

"Come now, Mr. Reed. A handsome man like yourself having free time—it's hard to believe. I'm certain you have many lady friends waiting in the wings."

John just about creamed his jeans and thought he'd better leave before frustration set in and he attacked her.

*   *   *

John's stomach told him it was lunchtime. He was afraid to stop at a restaurant for fear of missing Elaine's call, if she did call. So he stopped at a local deli for a container of chicken soup, a ham and cheese on rye, and a six-pack.

He finished lunch, turned on his opera, and with a can of beer he sat by the window, gazing at the clear blue sky.

The final record ended, which broke his trance. The first thing he must accomplish, since he was going on a vacation, was to purchase a new wardrobe and a new car, since the truck was a junker and it was too ugly for him to be driving around. Then a second thought occurred to him: Why buy a new car when he was going to Nassau? It would just sit around idly collecting dust. So the car was out.

He decided to take the bus into town and shop for a new wardrobe and then return by cab since he would probably have too many packages for the bus.

The ringing of the telephone interrupted his thoughts. In his anxiety to get it, thinking that it may be Elaine calling, he tripped over the footstool, falling on all fours and scraping both knees. He crawled to the phone and answered a caller who had the wrong number.

"Ah, screw you." He slammed the receiver back down. Now he was really pissed as he rubbed his knees. He took a shower and dressed casually, wearing gray slacks and a black pullover shirt and white sneakers. He checked his billfold to make certain that he had adequate funds for shopping.

With everything done that had to be done, he secured his apartment and walked out to the bus stop, arriving at the intersection at the same time as the bus. He took a seat by the window and watched the world go by.

When he arrived at Center City, the sidewalks were crowded with pedestrians and shoppers. John found Gimbals' Department store and headed directly to the men's department. The spring and summer fashions were on display. He browsed through the men's department until he found some clothing that appealed to him, and then he went on a buying spree, spending like a drunken sailor.

He began by purchasing two suits and a sports coat with matching trousers and all the accessories. His final purchase was a black tuxedo. The clerk could not be happier as he rang up the sales slips totaling a hefty twenty five hundred dollars.

Finally home, he placed the packages on the bed. Since he was still full of energy, and the trip only two days away, he decided to pack his bags. Using the two suitcases that he bought to transport the stolen money, he began packing.

The two suitcases worked out perfectly with the exception of his toilet articles and a few odds and ends that required the smaller suitcase he already had. He used a garment bag for his suits, sport coats, and trousers. He completed filling out his ID on the baggage tags furnished by Elaine and secured them on the luggage.

All set, he took a bottle of wine from the fridge and poured himself a glass, went to the living room, and sat in his easy chair with his eyes focused on the phone. He finally realized that she wasn't going to call. He sipped the wine as he looked down at the street and watched children playing street games. It was still too early for dinner, so he decided to relax a little longer. The thought of going to the Bahamas brought a smile to John's face. He rolled the wine glass across his forehead with both hands and thought to himself that he was on his way to a life of luxury. He finished every drop of the wine.

It was time for dinner. As he was cleaning up, his buddy Tony Renzi crossed his mind. "Yes. I'll have dinner at Tony's tonight."

Finished dressing, he left for Tony's restaurant for a steak dinner.

TONY'S RESTORANTE was a neighborhood bistro with good old-fashioned Italian-style home cooking. The restaurant had been owned and operated by Antonio and Rosa Renzi, until Antonio passed away two years ago. Tony Junior had taken over for his father. However, Rosa was still the boss. John knew just about every person in the place; he was greeted like a long lost brother.

"Hey, Tony! Look what the wind blew in! The Irishman from the East Side," yelled a waiter.

Young Tony, twenty-six, with a tall, medium build, black curly hair, and dark brown eyes, walked out from the kitchen and embraced John. They sat at the corner table and exchanged pleasantries.

"How is mamma Rosa doing, Tony? Is she still the chef?" John asked.

"What else? She'll die in that fucking kitchen," Tony answered.

They laughed, and Tony told John that he wouldn't tell her that he was here just yet. "She's behind on her orders. As you can see, there are many hungry people waiting for their food!"

"No problem," John said. Tony called the waitress over and ordered a bottle of wine and two glasses. He poured John's first. Then they raised their glasses and toasted, "Salute." As they drank, Tony asked him how things were going. "Great, Tony! Just great. In fact I'm going on vacation Saturday morning to the Bahamas." Before John could describe his vacation, word filtered to the kitchen that he was there, and Tony's mother rushed to greet him. John stood up, picked her up, held her in his arms, and kissed her cheeks. Tears were streaming from her eyes.

A customer seated at the bar asked the barkeeper, "What's all the fuss about over the guy who just arrived?"

"That's John Reed," the barkeeper answered.

"So what?"

The barkeeper told him to standby a second. "There's a waitress waiting to order drinks."

The barkeeper returned. "Five years ago Tony was dating a girl from the East Side. One night, while walking her home, some wise bastards began taunting him. He tried his best to control his temper, but when they started on his girl, he went into a rage and the battle began.

Being outnumbered five to one, Tony was losing the battle and getting hammered. That's when John happened along and witnessed Tony's crisis.

"He did not like the odds, so he jumped in to help Tony. He was doing a number on those punks when John took a knife in the gut. Finally the cops arrived. Tony and John were taken to the hospital. Tony was in serious condition, and the doctors feared the worst. They worked on him for three hours, and as you can see, he made it. The doctors were amazed. They credited John for saving Tony's life. If he hadn't come along when he did, Tony would not be alive today.

"Tony spent eight weeks in the hospital. John only had to spend three weeks in the hospital. He was lucky that the knife missed vital organs. He saved Tony's life, and John has been an adopted member of the family ever since. In fact, Tony's family financed John's trial for assault and armed robbery. It cost them big bucks. Unfortunately, he was found guilty and sent to prison for three to five years. Does that answer your question, wise ass?" The barkeeper paused for a second. "Funny thing, though. John is a hard person to understand at times."

"How's that?"

"He has a dual personality. Like, Jekyll and Hyde.

One minute, he's Mr. Good Guy. The next minute he'll turn on you with the slightest provocation. Hard guy to figure."

Envious, the guy again stared at John.

After regaining her composure, Mama told John that she would cook him an Italian special.

John gave Mama a frown.

"What's wrong, Johnny?" she asked. "I was thinking about a big juicy steak, Mama," John said meekly.

She looked at him. "Oh, you Irishmen! Steak, potatoes, and Irish stew."

They had a good laugh. Mama kissed John on the cheek.

"Okay, I make you a steak with the works."

John got his steak all right, and with the works. He began with a cup of Italian wedding soup, followed by a large antipasto, and ending with a Porterhouse steak that covered the entire plate. John struggled to consume the entire meal, which he had to do or face Mamma. He pushed his chair back from the table, put his two hands to his stomach, and then he loosened his belt.

Tony laughed. "So, what the hell have you been up to, John? You never stayed away from here this long. You had my mom worried that something may have happened to you. I lied telling her that you were working out-of-town, and I spoke with you everyday."

John pushed his chair back under the table and looked around and made certain that no one could listen. He leaned toward Tony.

"I made a big score, Tony. Big bucks." Again he looked around.

"Good for you, John. I'm happy for you." Of course, Tony did not ask who, why, or when.

John paused when more friends gathered at the table, and the drinking began. John got bombed out of his skull and passed out.

Tony's mother came in from the kitchen and saw John's condition and yelled at her son for letting John get so drunk.

"Don't worry, Mama." Tony laughed. "I'll see that he gets home okay."

He ordered a waiter to help put John in his car. Tony had a hard time; however, he managed to get John to bed. After John was settled under the covers, Tony opened the living room windows for fresh air. He thought, *now that John has money, he should get himself an air conditioner.*

He looked in on John who was stretched out and who appeared dead to the world. Tony laughed and sat for what he intended to be just a minute. However, he made the mistake of closing his eyes, and he soon dozed off.

Tony awoke and looked at his watch. It was two o'clock. Ready to leave, he took one last look at John and was tiptoeing to the door when John called his name. Surprised, he went to John's room.

"You were fast asleep a minute ago. You should be out like a light." Tony shook his head.

"I have a high recoup rate." John grinned. He took a bottle of wine from the refrigerator and two glasses and filled them to the brim.

"You have to be kidding," Tony said.

John ignored him and handed him a glass. They toasted each other and sat on the bed and drank.

"I have to get the hell home because morning comes mighty early, and I have a lot of things to do."

"You're the boss, John laughed. You can go in anytime."

"That's what you think. The boss has the hardest job."

"Okay. Finish your drink. I want to show you something before you leave."

Drinks consumed, John led Tony to the closet, placing a chair by the door. He told Tony to step up and remove the cover of the trap door.

"HOLY SHIT, John! You made more than a hit! You have the jackpot." Tony stepped down.

John stepped up and reached for a stack of bills, and he handed it to Tony.

"This is for mama. It should cover the lawyers' fees that she paid."

"There must be at least twenty-five G's here," Tony said excitedly. The lawyer's fees were only ten G's."

"Consider the extra cash as interest," John said.

Tony embraced John and thanked him.

John gave Tony an extra apartment key and told him to keep an eye on his money.

"Come over now and then and check out the place."

Tony took the key, looked down at the floor again, and looked up at John. "How do you follow an act like this?" Tony shook his head.

"You don't," John answered. "One more thing. Your place has a fine standing so I want to back up another restaurant, say, TONY'S II at a location you feel is reliable. I will only be a silent partner at fifty-fifty. Since I intend to live a soft, plush life, I want to be a capitalist and earn interest on my money. Capish?"

"Capish," Tony answered and put the key in his pocket. He kissed John on both cheeks and went back to work.

John yelled down the steps, "I'll send you a card from the Bahamas."

*   *   *

When Tony left, John went back to bed. Later, he awoke and sat on the edge of the bed to check the time. Eleven o'clock. He got up and drank some tomato juice very slowly. John was surprised that he was not hung over after all the wine he had consumed, but he was not complaining. He suddenly realized that he should notify "Mother Hubbard" that he was leaving for the Bahamas Saturday and give him the name and address of the hotel where he was staying.

He dialed Mr. Sherman's phone number. This time the receptionist answered.

"Good morning, Miss Winters, John Reed here. I made a special trip just to see you last week, and you were home loafing." John really laid it on.

She giggled. "If I knew you were coming, I would have come in," she said.

"I'll do that from now on," John told her. He then asked for Mr. Sherman.

"I'm sorry, Mr. Reed, but Mr. Sherman is at a meeting and will not return until two."

"That's fine. I'm leaving for the Bahamas Saturday morning for three weeks. Mr. Sherman wants the address of the hotel where I'll be staying. Would you see that he gets the address?" He furnished her the address of the Queen Ann Hotel.

"I'll pass it on. Thank you, Mr. Reed. Enjoy your vacation."

He hung up the phone, went to closet, and reached for a stack of bills, counting out fifty thousand dollars. He stacked the money in a shoebox and sealed the package.

Arriving at the post office, he handed the package to the postal clerk. John asked for the approximate time of delivery.

He was told three to four days. Satisfied, he left.

*   *   *

At Nine o'clock on Friday evening, John was performing a final check of his luggage when a knock on his door startled him.

Who in the hell could that be? he thought. He walked slowly to the door. "Who's there?"

"It's Sherman, Mr. Reed."

John opened the door to find Mr. Sherman with a second gentleman who turned out to be a detective. Sherman apologized and told John that he got his message about him going to the Bahamas Saturday morning.

"I thought that I'd stop by to wish you well."

John looked at the detective. "You brought him along to bid me farewell too?" John asked angrily.

Sherman apologized a second time and explained that it was procedure as he stared at the suitcases by the door.

John noticed his gaze. "Oh! Now I understand." He took the suitcase keys and tossed them to the detective.

"Okay. Check the fuckin' baggage and get the fuck out of my apartment." John went to the living room and turned on his aria, setting the volume to its highest pitch.

After a thorough search of the bags, the detective tossed the key on the floor at John's feet. Sherman told John that he would see him at the end of June and they left. His clothing was strewn about the floor.

"The bastards didn't even have the decency to put everything back."
John said to himself.

Suddenly, like a crazy, he burst out laughing. "The joke was on mother Hubbard, the fucker. He expected to find wads of money packed with my clothes but Johnny

Reed was way ahead of the bastard."

CHAPTER 9

Nine o'clock, coffee brewing, Pat Reardon arrived at the police station to be greeted by Chief Daniels.

Pat inhaled the aroma of coffee brewing. "If anything, Chief, you sure make a great cup of coffee."

Daniels thanked him as he filled Pat's cup to the brim. They sat back, relaxed, and sipped their coffee.

Reardon broke the silence. "Well chief, let's visit the waitress. She's our last resort. Maybe, just maybe, we can get lucky and she can give us some information about her encounter with the individuals Harris had mentioned."

Daniels called for his car and driver, and they left for Kay's apartment.

Kay opened the door a crack. Recognizing the chief, she opened the door all the way and invited him in.

After introducing Pat, Daniels and Kay sat on the sofa, while Pat sat on the easy chair.

Daniels began by explaining about the bank robbery.

"I know. Wasn't that awful? I'm happy that they didn't get away with it," Kay lied.

"I agree. However, three perished in the crash, but we believe that there were at least four men involved. We're hoping that you can shed some light on a few details regarding two individuals you had a problem with . . ."

"Oh. The two truckers?"

Pat joined in. "Were they truckers as you say?"

"Well, at least they said they were truckers driving through town. Horny to boot."

"Meaning?" Pat asked.

She looked at the Daniels who in turn nodded.

"Well . . . As I returned with their order one of them ran his hand up my leg. The rest officer Harris can explain."

"Was the diner crowded?" Pat asked.

"What do you mean?" she asked.

"What I'm getting at is: was is it possible that the diner was so crowded that three of four customers together had to sit at different tables?"

"Sorry Mr. Reardon. There was enough room to seat three to four customers at one table."

Realizing that they weren't getting anywhere, Pat asked, "Can you describe the truck drivers?"

Kay's description of Hal and Marty were precise.

Pat and Daniels looked at each other. Daniels thanked her and they left.

"She described two of thieves to a T, chief," Pat remarked as they drove to the station. Daniels made a new batch of coffee. He handed Pat a cup as they sat.

"Well, chief, I guess my job is finished here, so I'll return to headquarters tomorrow provided there is a flight available. I was hoping for better results . . . ."

Daniels looked at him and apologized.

"No need to apologize, Chief. That's the way it goes in our business. You win some; you lose some. So we'll chalk this one up as a loss." Reardon extended his hand to Daniels, thanking him for all his help.

* * *

John arrived at the travel agency at seven-fifty; Elaine was already waiting on the sidewalk with her luggage.

John got out of the cab and looked at her luggage.

"I didn't know that you were going on vacation for a year," he kidded.

"You should know how women are when they travel," she fired back.

"Sure," John answered, "everything but the kitchen sink."

The cab driver laughed as he watched the meter ticking away.

They needed the trunk and the entire back seat for their luggage, which meant that Elaine and John sat in the front seat.

John and the driver did not mind the tight squeeze, for John rubbed knees with Elaine. Her skirt was practically pulled up to her buns.

The poor driver was frustrated because he had to keep his eyes on the road and could not take full advantage of the scenery.

John loved it. She noticed and tried her best to adjust her skirt but did so with little success.

Elaine opened her purse and took out an envelope containing John's contract and airline tickets.

As she handed them to John, she said, "Please don't lose these." He secured the envelope in his coat pocket, drawing attention to his coat. Elaine looked him over and told him that he looked handsome.

"So do you. So do you," he said, staring at her legs.

"Oh, you men are all alike," she said, blushing.

Suddenly, John realized that the cab driver was taking the long way to the airport.

"Is this the best way to the airport?" he asked.

"It's a short cut," the cabby answered.

"A short cut my ass," John shot back, angrily. "We should have been at the airport fifteen minutes ago." John directed him from that point on.

Arriving at the airport, they unloaded the baggage and John gave the cabby the exact change.

"No tip?" The cabby asked.

John put his arm around his shoulder and walked him to the front of the cab and said, "I'll give you five seconds to get in the fuckin' cab and beat it or I'll bash your face inside out."

John gave him the Mr. Hyde stare. The cabby looked into John's eyes. Shock and fear appeared on his face. He immediately got into the cab and sped off with the door ajar. Fortunately Elaine did not hear or see John's anger.

*   *   *

The flight took off on schedule. The captain welcomed them aboard, and with the customary explanation: "Flying altitude of 35,000 feet. The weather in New York is perfect with clear skies and temperatures in the mid-seventies. Flight time to New York would be approximately two and one half hours. Enjoy your flight, everyone."

After three drinks John fell asleep.

He awoke when plane impacted the ground upon touchdown. Opening his eyes, he looked toward Elaine. "Did we?"

She answered that they did and that he had sawed a lot of lumber during the entire flight. They laughed.

*   *   *

Kennedy Airport. What a sight. John whistled as he looked around.

"Wow. I thought O'Hare Airport was big."

Elaine broke his trance and told him that they should pick up their luggage. John took her hand and quickly followed the signs to the baggage terminal.

They arrived in time to find their luggage the only pieces remaining on the conveyer belt. John was embarrassed. With the help of a skycap they arrived at ground transportation level. Elaine mentioned that there was bus service available that went directly to the New York harbor and that the rates were reasonable.

"I'm on vacation and I'm not sparing any expense. I'm not rubbing elbows with other people in an airport limo," he told her.

He signaled an oversized cab whose driver rushed over and started loading their luggage. Elaine was stunned.

"Do you realize how far the Port of New York is from the airport? It's going to cost a fortune," she told John.

"Who cares? I'll tell you a second time I am not sparing any cost on my vacation," he said.

She could only shake her head in disbelief.

They had enough room to sit comfortably in the back seat. John told the driver to turn on soft music and put his arm around Elaine's shoulder. She happened to turn her head toward John to say something, and as he turned to listen their lips met.

"WOW!" John said. "Let's do that one more time!"

She told him that he was crazy and a fast worker.

"Well, at least I'm a happy crazy," he answered.

*   *   *

New York City. The huge skyscrapers mesmerized John. One could not believe that he was from a big city like Chicago. Instead, he acted like a kid from the foothills of Kentucky. They drove through downtown Manhattan and the heart of Broadway.

The cabby drove directly to dock side. He unloaded the luggage onto a ship's platform luggage carts. John and Elaine handed their tickets to a ship's porter.

John asked the cabby the fare cost. For a second Elaine thought that John would want her to share the expense.

"One hundred and eighty dollars," the cabby responded. John gave him two one hundred dollar bills and four twenty-dollar bills.

The driver just about shit his pants. He thanked John, got in his cab, and headed back to the airport to look for another Johnny Reed.

Elaine was relieved that she did not have to contribute to the fare, and she admired John for that. He scored a top ten with her, as they walked arm-in-arm up the ship's gangplank.

*   *   *

They entered the main deck to a celebration. People were everywhere with champagne glasses in one hand and bottles of champagne in the other. They were dancing to the music of roaming musicians.

When John looked around the ship in awe, Elaine realized that this was his first cruise. She leaned forward so that he could hear above the noise and told him that this was procedure for the first day of the cruise.

"It's called a 'Bon Voyage' party," she said.

Finally, the ship's horn unleashed a loud burst, signaling that the ship was preparing to get underway. The loudspeaker informed friends and relations who were not assigned to the cruise to exit the ship immediately.

The booze added fuel to John's excitement. Elaine noticed and told him that they should check into their rooms and get settled.

John immediately took her by the arm, and they were on their way.

She was on the main deck John was two decks below, which disappointed him. He was hoping to be closer to her cabin.

His disappointment showed and she noticed.

"Don't be discouraged," she said. "You'll spend more time on deck than in your room, because there are a lot of activities going on."

"Hell. I'd rather spend more time in my room with you." He grinned and escorted her to her cabin. He wanted to enter, but she thought better of it and told him that she needed to unpack.

"I'll check dining arrangements and table assignment. I'll call you and you can pick me up for dinner." She slowly nudged him out of the door.

*   *   *

The cruise ship was underway. John unpacked his bags. He lay on the bed for what he supposed would be a short nap.

The ringing of the phone awakened him. He answered, and it was Elaine.

"Well are you going to sleep the night away?" she asked.

He apologized and asked the time.

"Dinner time," she answered. "We are scheduled for the first seating.

"Are you ready?" he asked.

"I've been ready," she said.

"I'll be there in ten minutes," John said.

John decided to wear his tuxedo.

Elaine was waiting with the cabin door open.

When John arrived and saw her standing there, her beauty immediately mesmerized him. She was dressed in a blue, low-cut dress that displayed her well-endowed bust. The hem of the dress was high above her knees. Her blond hair was stacked high.

"Sheer beauty," he said, as he kept looking her up and down. In fact, he walked around her twice.

"Well, say something," she said.

"If I spoke what I'm thinking, I'd be in the doghouse for the remainder of the trip," he told her.

She couldn't top that, so she changed the subject by telling him that he looked handsome and sexy himself.

John took her arm and led her to the door. "We better get going before things get out of hand."

*   *   *

John and Elaine were seated at their designated dinner table. The captain began making his rounds to meet and greet the guests. Stopping at their table, he introduced himself to John and Elaine, holding Elaine's hand longer than normal, which was a mistake, causing Dr. Jekyll to transform into Mr. Hyde. If stares could kill, the captain would have died that precise moment. John's eyes reflected hatred and rage.

Elaine became frightened. She looked into John's eyes and a chill passed through her body. She quickly withdrew her hand from the captain's hand and, again, saw that evil look as John's eyes followed the captain, who was moving toward the other guests. She took John's hand in hers, leaned forward, and kissed his cheek to settle him down.

It worked. John transformed back to Mr. Nice Guy as she handed him a menu, but she could not take her eyes away from his.

John realized that he had screwed up. He poured her a glass wine. He proposed a toast to her that she acknowledged. Meanwhile the food arrived and they ate.

Afterward they walked to the lounge for an after-dinner drink. The band was playing soft romantic music, and John thought a dance was in order. They danced cheek-to-cheek. Although he held her close, she snuggled even closer.

They danced and drank the night away. John was becoming impatient. All he could think about was getting Elaine in bed. The drinks finally caught up to Elaine; instead of dancing she was now staggering across the dance floor.

John clutched her arm and they returned to Elaine's cabin. He took her cabin key from her purse and unlocked the door as he struggled to keep her from falling to the floor. He opened the door, and with his help, Elaine staggered to the bed and did a free fall, landing on her back. In doing so, she exposed her legs and thighs, allowing him a full view of her heavenly body.

He removed his coat and kicked off his shoes. He hurriedly removed his shirt and trousers. He quickly undressed her. The love scene began.

Elaine had barely caught her breath when John was back at her a second time. The lovemaking completed, they drifted off to sleep.

* * *

Elaine was the first to wake-up. She leaned over to look at her watch. It was ten o'clock. She opened the curtain and let the sunlight fill the room. She quickly made up her face and fixed her hair and put on a pair of white shorts, a multicolor tank top, and white sneakers.

She placed a note on her pillow informing John that she had gone to the main deck and the swimming pool for breakfast.

Meanwhile John awoke and ran his hand over her side of the bed and immediately realized she was not in bed. He searched the cabin and found the note. He quickly dressed and rushed to his cabin. He changed into a pair of white shorts and a silk pink shirt, buttoning only the last four buttons in order to reveal his bare chest. He headed for the pool to find Elaine.

He found her all right, sitting on a beach chair talking with two guys, and she appeared to be enjoying their company. He walked briskly toward them. When he arrived, she greeted him, and he returned her greeting while he stared at the two guys with his evil eye. The two excused themselves and scurried away.

Again, Elaine had seen fire in John's eyes. However, she did not want to show any emotion at the present time. She took John by the hand, and led him to the pool. They sat at the edge of the pool with their feet hanging in the water, holding hands and taking in the sun. John's apparent short temper was heavy on Elaine's mind.

"We had enough sun for the day," Elaine told John. "It's time to have brunch."

John used two plates because he wanted to sample a little of everything. Elaine shook her head. "You're a hard person to understand, John Reed."

He grinned and continued eating his food.

* * *

The next two days, John was like a kid on his first journey to the circus. He had never dreamed that things like this existed. When he had been a kid, growing up on the East Side of Chicago, the fire hydrant was his swimming pool and playing street games was his vacation.

The evening before docking in Nassau, the ship's social director prepared fun and games, music and dancing on the main deck. Of course, food was included. Tables and tables of the best food imaginable lined the entire main deck. The menu included whole lobster and lobster tail. Again, John ate like there was no tomorrow. Elaine was enjoying herself watching John eat. They managed a few dances in between courses. The only thing that stopped John from gorging himself was the break for fun and games. Afterward, they danced some more.

John finally called time-out and invited Elaine for a stroll on deck. There was a chill in the air, and, with the strapless dress she was wearing, Elaine developed cold shoulders. John noticed and immediately took off his coat and draped it around her. They leaned on the rail and looked up at the cloudless sky. A full moon streaked a silvery beam across the ocean. He held her close and kissed her cheek. He glanced at his watch and thought it was time to return to her cabin.

They hit the bed simultaneously and landed on their backs, undressing each other. They stared into each other's eyes before the lovemaking began, ending with her scream of ecstasy, which left John's ears ringing.

John asked what time the ship was scheduled to dock in the morning.

"Nine. Why did you ask?"

"I want to be on deck when the ship sails into the harbor."

"Oh shit," she said as she jumped from the bed and slipped into her robe. "I must pack a bag to take to the hotel." Packing one bag, she told him that he should also pack his luggage since he wasn't making the return trip.

He agreed and kissed her and was off to his cabin to pack his bags.

After packing, John felt exhausted from the night's activities, so he decided to take a short nap. He called the desk for a wake-up call for seven-thirty.

The clerk laughed because it was already six o'clock, "Yes, sir, seven-thirty it is." John fell back to sleep.

When the wake-up call came, John answered, "Sure. Sure. Good morning to you too."

He looked for clothes to wear when he realized he had already packed everything. "You stupid fuck, John," he said aloud. "If you had a brain, you'd be dangerous."

Unlocking one suitcase—luckily the right one—he found a pair of dark blue shorts, a white tank top, white socks, and a pair of white sneakers.

He called for baggage pickup and went to Elaine's cabin.

"Let's go on the main deck for a light breakfast," he suggested.

"A light breakfast? I bet." she replied.

John surprised her. He had scrambled eggs and black coffee. She was satisfied with just toast, grapefruit, and coffee.

They joined the other guests on the main deck as the ship maneuvered dockside with the aid of two tugboats.

The "Welcome to the Bahamas" celebration began: confetti, streamers, and champagne. The steel band played their native music on the dock.

John missed the announcement "All ashore who are going ashore" that was made over the loudspeaker because he was leaning over the rail mesmerized by all the celebration.

Elaine had to lead him by the hand down the gangway.

She arranged with the ship's stewards to have their baggage delivered to the Queen Ann Hotel.

There just happened to be a cab standing by. Elaine directed the driver to the Queen Ann hotel.

*   *   *

Elaine checked into the hotel for one night and then walked to the gift shop to browse while she waited for John to check in.

John, greeted by the desk clerk, immediately asked about his package.

The clerk stared at John, confused, and apologized. "Sorry, sir, there is no package for a Mr. Reed."

"What do you mean, no package for Mr. Reed?" he shouted loud enough so that everyone in the lobby heard him. "Is this some kind of joke?"

He turned to see people staring at him, including Elaine.

Embarrassed, he turned his attention back to the clerk and whispered, "There was a package sent to this hotel addressed to me a few days ago."

The clerk became upset and turned to look for the manager for help.

The manager had already noticed and walked to the desk. He approached John, and before the clerk could explain the problem, a mail person walked to the desk.

"Hey maaan, I forgot this one." John immediately noticed that the mail person held his package, and John was relieved. The clerk smiled happily and handed him the package.

John took the package and offered the clerk and the manager a weak smile. He reached in his pocket and took out two twenty-dollar bills and gave them to the clerk. "I hope that this makes up for my rude behavior." Of course, to the local people, the American dollar was a panacea for anything and everything.

*   *   *

He placed the package under his arm and hurried to the elevator, but Elaine was gone. "Ah fuck. I bet she's pissed."

He took the elevator to his floor and went to his room. He placed the carton on the bed and proceeded to look for a safe hiding place. After ten minutes, he noticed an air-conditioning duct in the ceiling.

Perfect, he thought. He required a screwdriver to remove the vent cover. He looked around and he saw a letter opener on the desk. He took it and a chair to the duct's location and removed the vent cover. He took ten thousand dollars from the carton and placed the carton inside the vent.

With that project completed, he began thinking of ways to reconcile with Elaine. A knock at the door broke his concentration. It was the bellhop with his baggage.

*   *   *

Elaine was sitting on the patio overlooking the ocean as the warm breeze teased her hair. She watched as the huge waves pounded the beach. It reminded her of John's terrible temper and his crazy antics and the way his attitude changed from one day to the next. One minute he was great, the next he underwent a complete change of personality. *Eventually he is going to explode*, she thought. Then she wondered how long and how much she could put up with his antics. She stood up, and took one final look at the ocean and returned to her room.

*   *   *

John's short nap ended being a five-hour sleep, and it took banging on his door to wake him. Startled, he got out of bed and walked to the door scratching his head.

He opened the door to find Elaine standing with her arms folded, and she was clearly pissed.

He smiled; she didn't. She told him that she should be angry, not him.

He looked at her and laughed.

"What gave you the idea that I was angry with you?" he said.

"It's six o'clock, and you did not even bother calling me about dinner."

"Hell. I thought that you were angry with me for yelling in the lobby. When I got to the elevator, you were gone. So I went to my room and decided to take a quick nap; as you can see it turned into a long sleep."

He invited her in and looked her up and down. She was wearing, white short shorts, and a pink, see-through blouse.

"You know that you have a perfect set of legs?" Then he decided to try to pick up a few points that he desperately needed at this point in time, asking, "Now, what's your pleasure?"

"I would like to sight-see the hotel before dinner. I heard that there is a casino here."

"You mean casino-casino? As in gambling?"

"Something like that, yes," she answered.

"Well, let's go. I'm ready and rearing' to go," he told her. She ignored him and changed the subject, "What was commotion that you created in the hotel lobby this morning?"

"Just a misunderstanding with the clerk about a parcel I sent myself containing paper work that I have to complete in the next few days," John lied. He cut the subject short by telling her that if she wanted to travel around the hotel, they had better get going.

It took him exactly ten minutes to dress. He wore a pair of black slacks and a white silk shirt.

They proceeded to Elaine's room so that she could dress. She chose a white skirt and light blue blouse with a blue scarf.

They were off for the grand tour of the hotel. They stopped at every restaurant on the way as they checked out the various menus. They lastly selected a restaurant and had a light supper.

Afterward, they continued their tour. John began complaining that his feet were beginning to ache and directed her to the hotel lounge for a drink. They ordered their usual drinks and watched a musical combo on stage above the bar.

After three hours and many drinks, John became numb. As for Elaine, she was also feeling no pain.

They forgot about the casino, went directly to her room, and climbed into bed. John immediately fell asleep.

Elaine looked at him and laughed while she took off his shoes and covered him with the bedspread. She undressed and climbed into bed beside him.

John woke up first. He looked over and saw Elaine fast asleep and stark naked. Seeing her nude body was all John needed. He immediately attacked her before she realized what was happening. Unfortunately, it didn't last long enough for John's satisfaction.

John realized that she wasn't too happy being attacked, so he suggested brunch. "After brunch, we'll gamble awhile and win spending money for you," John told her.

That hit home with her. She recommended that he return to his room and dress while she did the same. This would save time. John agreed and left.

John dressed and returned to her room. They made a remarkable couple. In fact, they turned many heads walking through the hotel lobby on the way.

After brunch, they were both feeling uncomfortable because of over-eating. John ordered two cordials to help settle their stomachs, and it worked. The long walk to the casino also helped. Elaine paused, looked around the casino, and was awed by the various gaming tables and the thousands and thousands of lights decorating the entire casino. There was the hustle and bustle of people roaming around the various gaming tables.

After a quick tour, John led her to the craps table. She appeared embarrassed and told him that she knew nothing about gambling.

"Just watch me and observe the people standing around the table. You'll learn in no time," John assured her.

John put a thousand dollars on the table in exchange for chips.

Elaine just about died when she saw the ten one hundred dollar bills. She watched in awe as John began placing chips on various numbers; at the same time she studied the people as they tossed the dice.

John was holding his own when he was given the dice for his turn to toss the dice.

He told Elaine to pick up the dice and toss them like the others had done.

Embarrassed again, she refused. "I can't," she said.

"Toss the dice," he demanded.

Now the other people at the table were getting impatient.

"Come on, sweetie, toss em, toss, em. We don't have all day."

Her first two tosses were a disaster: the dice bounced off the table into the crowd.

Now the other players were upset and asked for a new shooter. Elaine agreed with them.

John, infuriated by their remarks, told her that she was the shooter and stared angrily at the other players who suddenly became silent. Elaine stood frozen with dice in hand.

Since she had known John, Elaine had noticed that whenever he stared angrily at people, or raised his voice, he got everyone's attention.

This time he spoke softly. "Toss the dice gently and make certain that they hit the back of the table."

On her third toss she closed her eyes. She heard everyone yell, and she looked at John and asked what had happened. He told her that she tossed an eleven and won. Well, she went on to make twelve passes in a row. Now the table was really jumping, and of course John was raking in the chips.

Elaine finally rolled a seven, ending her turn. This time all the players and even a few observers applauded. She had no idea what was winning or losing, but John had stacks of one hundred dollar chips.

After three hours of playing, John called it quits. Using both hands, he gathered his chips and they went to the cashier's gage.

After totaling the chips the cashier handed John a stack of five hundred dollar bills. He turned to Elaine and gave her a stack of bills and said, "Since you did such a great job, the money is yours to keep."

Elated, Elaine flashed a huge smile. Elaine was so excited that she hugged John and kissed him.

John thought that they could use a drink right about now, so they went to the lounge. There happened to be an all-male Japanese combo playing and singing, of all things, country and western music. They were about to be seated when John noticed that she was still clutching the money in her hand.

John laughed. "Let me hold your money for safe keeping until we get back to your room," he said.

"You are giving it back to me, aren't you?" she kidded.

John just ignored her and ordered bourbon on the rocks for himself and a Bloody Mary for her.

The entertainment was terrific, considering the group was from Japan and playing country music. They topped off the evening in her room with the usual lovemaking.

On Elaine's last evening in port, she recommended an early dinner so she could pack her bags and go to bed early.

They were resting in bed when she turned on her side toward John. Her chin supported by her right hand, she told him that she was sorry that it was all coming to an end.

He answered that she did not have to return so soon. She could stay as long as she wished.

Elaine sat up and looked at him. "You mean?"

"You got it," John answered.

Elaine stared at him with her mouth opened. She did not know what to say.

"What about my business?" she asked.

He laughed and said, "That's your problem."

"You're a big help."

Elaine thought for a moment. "I would have to return to Chicago and arrange with an answering service to take all calls. I can return sometime Tuesday, if there is a flight available." She stared at John.

Without hesitating, John called the airline and confirmed a nine o'clock flight from Chicago to Nassau Tuesday. He then asked the agent if there was a direct flight to Chicago available tomorrow.

He was told that all flights were booked for Saturday. However, there was a flight available at three o'clock in first-class on Sunday afternoon.

"Sold," John said, confirming the reservation.

"You're set. Now we can spend the entire day together Saturday." She was flabbergasted.

"Brother, you really move fast. One more thing, I must notify the cruise director I'm not returning with the cruise ship."

"Go." John handed her the phone.

After making her call, she leaned back. "I need a drink."

Again, without hesitating, John called room service and ordered drinks. John then ordered a rental car for twelve o'clock Sunday. "We'll use it for the trip to the airport," John said.

He paused and continued, "I know that something else will cross your mind eventually. So, I'll tell you in advance how I can afford to do what I do. I'm a stockbroker and a silent partner in a restaurant business."

She was impressed.

Meanwhile, their drinks had arrived, and after finishing their beverages, they fell asleep.

Elaine was the first to wake up. She showered and put on her white bikini.

When John awoke to turn and see her sitting at the dresser in her bikini, the blood rushed to his loins.

He sat up on the edge of the bed and asked her to sit beside him.

"No way. I want to have breakfast and spend the day on the beach," she answered.

John made a move toward her, but Elaine was too fast and hurried to the bathroom and locked the door. John begged for her to open the door, but Elaine refused. Realizing that it was a lost cause, he asked, "How about letting me in to shower and shave, please?"

"Not unless you promise not to attack me if I open the door."

John promised. She let him in. After his shower and shave, they left for the beach. But that evening, there was no arguing: they went at it hot and heavy.

The next morning, Elaine woke up first and leaned over to check the time. "Shit! John, it's eleven-ten. I have to get ready." She hurried to the bathroom to take a shower.

Showered and dressed, she completed her packing and called room service to have her luggage picked up and placed in the hotel lobby.

All the time John was on the bed watching her run around like a nut.

"Boy, you're a big help."

"Okay. What can I do to help?" he asked.

She did not answer but looked at her watch again. It was twelve-twenty. "The least you could do is make a reservation for breakfast or lunch," she said.

John checked with the desk and found that there was a Sunday brunch already in progress ending at two o'clock.

With reservations confirmed, they arrived at the dining room and were escorted to their table by the maitre d'. There was wall-to-wall food. A piano player was entertaining the customers. While eating and enjoying the pianist, Elaine suddenly realized that she had left her makeup kit in her room. She asked John to please fetch the kit. "I believe that I left it on the sink."

"What do you mean, 'fetch'? I'm not a dog," John kidded.

"Go. Go," she demanded.

John kissed her cheek and left to run his errand.

He was stopped on the way by the desk clerk, who recognized him as the man who had raised hell about the package the first day of his arrival. He also remembered the large tip John had given him as an apology.

"Are you enjoying his vacation, sir?"

John offered a quick "okay" and continued to his room.

The desk clerk delaying him, coupled with a slow elevator and a problem locating Elaine's compact, resulted in the elapse of twenty minutes.

Elaine wondered what was keeping John as she looked at her watch.

A gentleman sitting at the bar noticed her sitting alone. He picked up his drink and walked slowly toward her and said, "How can someone as lovely as you be dining alone?"

Before she could explain that she wasn't alone, he took her hand and escorted her to the dance floor. She did not want to create a scene, so she danced with him.

This guy has balls, she thought, hoping and praying prayed that the song would end before John returned.

No such luck. John indeed had returned and immediately noticed her dancing with the guy. He stood at the entrance until the song ended.

However, the man insisted on another dance.

John walked across the dance floor and took hold of the guy's wrist.

"How about dancing with me, asshole?" John bit his tongue.

Elaine was really scared. She tried to explain that the guy didn't realize she wasn't alone.

John did not hear a word Elaine said. With two quick right hands, one to the stomach and the other to the jaw, he floored the guy. John picked him up by his coat lapels and struck him again, sending him sprawling across the floor.

The police arrived and put John in a waiting police car. He saw Elaine hurrying to a waiting cab.

He tried breaking away from the police, but he could not fight off all three. He was then struck on the head with a police baton, rendering him unconscious.

Awaking to the real world John found himself in jail.

He was given a cold, wet cloth to put against the sore spot on his head.

"Well, fuck head," he said to himself, "you did it again. Maybe you deserve to be in jail." Sitting on a bunk, he leaned back against the cell wall. The jailer brought him aspirin and a cup of coffee. He thanked him and asked the condition of the guy he had assaulted. He was told that the gentlemen was in the hospital with a broken jaw and a possible concussion.

"Shit. That's bad news for me, ain't it?"

The jailor stared at him for a second and replied, "Very bad news for you."

John discarded the aspirin and opted for the coffee. Clutching the cup with both hands, his thoughts quickly turned to Elaine. He knew that he was up the creek without a paddle this time.

He lay down on the bunk thinking that he was not going to beat this rap since the guy he assaulted was in the hospital, and he soon dozed off.

John was startled when he awoke to see a tall, thin, distinguished gentleman neatly dressed standing before him.

"May I?" the man asked.

John moved over on his bunk and made room for the gentleman to sit.

John did not say a word and just stared at him and wondered if he were dreaming. The_____gentleman did not introduce himself. He said that he represented the hotel. He went on to explain that the hotel would like to keep the incident out of the local papers. In_____addition, John could continue to be a guest at the hotel for as long as he wished.

"What do you have in mind?" John asked.

The man paused, stared into his eyes, and said he had a solution that would settle the case and set him free.

Without hesitating John answered back, "Name it."

"All you would have to do is pay the hospital expenses and make a cash settlement with the man you hit, and you are a free man."

"How much?" John asked.

"Including my fee, the total cost would be thirty-thousand dollars."

John went into an acting routine as though he were pondering the offer.

"You got it, but you will have to wait two or three days, since I don't have that kind of cash with me." John did not want this guy to know he carried a sizeable amount of cash.

"That is fine. I expect the money by Tuesday afternoon to be left at the hotel lobby." He bid John farewell and left.

John stopped him. "Hey. When do I get out?"

The gentleman turned, looked at John, and said, "Patience, my good fellow, patience."

Hours later John was still in jail. *This guy may be a wacko*, he thought.

Before he could worry any more, the jailor returned and opened the cell door. "You are free to go, sir," he said.

John picked up his belongings at the front desk on the way out. He hurried back to the hotel hoping that Elaine hadn't left for the airport yet.

The hotel doorman confirmed that she had taken a cab to the airport.

Upset, he returned to his room. He packed a small bag then checked with the airline for a flight Monday to Chicago.

There was a flight scheduled for two o'clock Monday afternoon that he immediately confirmed. He then went to the hotel lounge and started on his bourbon and water. After four hours of continued drinking and without food, he felt no pain. He staggered to the elevator to his room.

The early morning sun flashed a ray of light directly in his eyes. He used his arm to shield his eyes.

Elaine immediately crossed his mind, so he was up for the duration. He leaned over to check the clock, which showed eight. He was trying to sit up when the pain streaked across his forehead. He placed the palm of his hand on his forehead and lay back down on the bed. He reached for the phone to call room service for tomato juice and black coffee.

The tomato juice and coffee seemed to do the trick. Feeling a lot better, he took a cold shower and shaved. He dressed and went to the hotel dining room. However, the smell of food nauseated him, so he ordered a container of black coffee to go and drank it in the lobby. He ordered a second cup to go, which he drank as he walked the hotel grounds. He walked to the beach and sat along the water's edge.

Without his realizing it, the walk had taken him approximately five miles from the hotel. He decided to sit on the beach and rest. Fortunately, he still had the newspaper in hand and used it for a blanket.

As he sat in the cool morning breeze and warm bright sun, he surveyed the ocean and the beach. John was amazed that the beach was so crowded with people that early in the morning. They were already enjoying the sun and the ocean.

In fact, he noticed a redhead staring in his direction a short distance away. She was smiling as she lay on her stomach with her bra loosened, her breasts pressed against the sand. She was attractive, John thought. He acknowledged the redhead with a nod of his head.

She stood up, brushing the sand from her body. It looked as though she were going to walk in his direction. Unfortunately, John had an afternoon flight to catch. He stood up, took a last look at the ocean, and returned to his hotel.

Upon arriving in his room, he went directly to where the funds were stashed. He took thirty-two thousand dollars and hurried to the lobby.

John approached the front desk and told the clerk, "I'll be returning to Chicago today, and possibly returning Tuesday evening. Hold my room and record all calls and messages." He then asked the clerk for a large envelope and a pen. He placed the thirty thousand in the envelope and sealed it. He wrote his name across the front and asked for the manager.

The manager came immediately and greeted him. John handed him the envelope. "Someone will be looking for me or this envelope Tuesday. You are to give it to that person." John paused. "You know, I don't even know the guy's name."

With a devilish grin the manager seemed to understand almost as if he were expecting the envelope.

John laughed. "I should have known that the hotel was involved." He gave the manager two twenty-dollar bills: twenty for him and twenty for the desk clerk. The manager thanked him.

John then went to the coffee shop and ordered a hamburger and coffee. He finished in time to go to the airport. After paying his check, he walked to the lobby entrance and asked the doorman for a cab. There happened to be a cab waiting curbside. The driver got out and ran up to John. Taking his bag, the driver flashed a huge smile that reflected missing teeth. John laughed. It had been a while since he had been given a reason to laugh. He was off to the airport.

*   *   *

Four o'clock. Chief Daniels began his meeting with his staff.

"Okay, what do we have?" he asked, directing his attention to inspector Sheen.

"Well, sir, it appears that every bank employee we screened was beyond suspicion, each being a long-time employee with outstanding records . . ."

Daniels hesitated before asking, "You mean not one blemish?"

There was a moment of silence, then inspector Sheen turned to Daniels and said, "There is one item that may seem odd, sir."

"That is?"

"Mr. Jackson, one of the bank tellers, recently purchased a late model automobile . . ."

"Well, we can't be concerned about him since he was killed a week or two ago. Is that all you could come up with, inspector?"

"That's it, sir."

"Thank you, gentlemen. I think that we can end the investigation. I'll notify Pat—ah, Mr. Reardon."

*   *   *

"Mr. Jackson, a teller, was the only possible suspect my inspector could come up with."

"Was?" Pat repeated.

"He was involved in a car accident that killed him."

"Um, interesting," Pat said. "A bank employee, eh? What type of accident may I ask?"

"DUI. His alcohol limit was at its highest."

"It sure is a coincidence that a bank employee of a bank that was just robbed has been killed."

"I'm afraid so, Pat."

Scratching his chin, Pat turned to Daniels and asked, "Is it possible that Jackson was murdered and it was made to look like an accident?"

"Not according to the coroner."

"I've known coroner's to be wrong." Pat grinned. He paused and asked Daniels if it would be possible to check Jackson's personal effects at the bank.

"I don't see why not," Daniel's answered. "However, I'm certain that his personal belongings were given to his wife. But I'll check first thing in the morning and let you know."

"Good," Pat said before leaving.

*   *   *

John opened the door to a musty-smelling apartment. As he entered, he stepped on more advertising flyers that read "First, second, and third notice" in bold letters. He picked up the flyers and tossed them into the trashcan. He opened the windows for fresh air.

Bags unpacked, he made himself comfortable. He went to the fridge for a bottle of wine, poured himself a glass, and turned on his phonograph to opera. Then he sat by the window drinking wine and watching the kids as they played street games.

After two full glasses of wine, he dozed off. He awoke as the last record was finishing. Still feeling the jet lag, he went to bed.

John slept the entire night and part of the next morning. Upon waking, he leaned over and looked at his watch. It was ten-thirty. "Time to rise and shine," he said to himself. He dressed in an old pair of blue denim shorts, a tee shirt, and loafers before leaving.

*   *   *

John was hungry for breakfast, so he walked to Tony's Ristorante. He found Tony working on the day's menu.

"Hey, John," Tony yelled as they embraced. "How was the vacation? I see no tan except some neon burn."

"It was great, Tony. I had a great time," John answered. "I'll probably be returning in a day or two." He then asked for Mama.

"Hell, I forgot to tell you the last time you were here. She was planning a trip to the old country for the last five years. She finally decided to go and is already on her way to visit her sister and old friends."

"Who's going to make my favorite breakfast?" John asked.

"No problem," Tony answered. "I'll make it for you. In fact, I can use some breakfast myself."

It took Tony approximately twenty minutes to prepare the meal.

They sat down to eat. Tony told him that when they finished their meal, he was going to show John something. When they finished eating, Tony reminded the headwaiter that the dining room must be prepared and ready for the noon meal. He then led John to his car.

"Where we going?" John asked.

"The west side," Tony answered.

After driving for twenty minutes, they came to an intersection. Tony stopped the car.

"Well?" John asked.

"Over there, you stupid fuck," Tony kidded. He pointed to a building being renovated and almost completed.

John looked and was surprised when he saw the sign: JOHNNY AND TONY'S II RISTORANTE.

"Wow," was all John could say, as he got out of the car and followed Tony to the front entrance of the building.

The builders were hard at work, completing the final stages of the kitchen and dining room.

"It's beautiful, Tony!" John said.

Tony told him that they would have the grand opening in three weeks.

"I thought that you were going to use your name only," John said. "Not knowing me or my name and all."

"Nah, no problem, John. They will get to know your name in no time."

John, being facetious, asked if there were ample money to cover the project.

Tony stared at him for a second. "You got to be shitting me, John!"

John laughed and said, "Yes, I'm kidding."

Tony's quote of one hundred and forty thousand dollars, including all the furniture, made John happy, but he could really care less. Cash was no problem. Nevertheless, he thanked Tony as they walked back to the car.

Back at the restaurant, they sat in the dining room as the other kitchen and dinning personnel were about to set up for the noon meal.

Tony picked up a bottle of wine and two glasses and returned to the table. They toasted their new business.

Tony then noticed that something was troubling John.

"Okay, John. I've known you a long time so I know when something is troubling you."

John shook his head, and then explained his meeting and relationship with Elaine.

He did not elaborate on the sexy stuff.

"Hell, John, with your money and great looks, she'll come around. Besides, from where I'm sitting, you can have any young woman your heart desires."

John finished his glass of wine. He stood up and embraced Tony, saying, "I'm looking forward to the grand opening. I'll see you in a couple of weeks."

Tony bid John "Ciao."

*   *   *

On his way back to his apartment, John wanted to run to Elaine's agency, but he didn't want to show that he was overly anxious to see her.

Arriving home, he immediately poured himself a glass of wine, turned on his opera, and hoped that the wine and the music would help him fall asleep so that he would not have to think about Elaine. But he couldn't sleep; in fact, he got up from his chair, changed clothes, and was off to Elaine's agency.

She was in her office, confirming John's suspicion that she had no intention of returning to the Bahamas.

He entered the agency and walked toward her. She glanced up and noticed him but did not flinch as she continued speaking to a customer sitting by her desk. There was also another couple waiting to speak with her.

John walked to a small table displaying vacation brochures and browsed through them.

Twenty minutes elapsed and the customer was still speaking with her. Now John was getting angry. Finally, the customer thanked her and left.

The couple started toward Elaine. John cut in front of them and led them to the door and told them to come back in thirty minutes. They saw that Mr. Hyde look in John's eyes, and they left.

Elaine ran toward him and yelled that he was screwing up her business.

He took her by the arm and led her to her chair, sat her down, and placed a thousand dollars on her desk.

"This is for that last couple. If they don't come back, you didn't lose anything.

Why didn't you return to the Bahamas as planed?" John asked.

She looked at him angrily. "I have no intention of returning to Nassau with you."

He paused to gather his thoughts before saying, "We were doing great. You said so yourself."

"That was before I realized you are a raving maniac," she yelled as she turned her face toward the window.

John paused and again apologized for acting stupid.

"Sure. Every time you go crazy, you apologize. Well, I warned you that the next time would be the last. So get out of my life now."

He held her hand to his lips and tried desperately to persuade her to give him one more chance, with the usual promise that he'd change and never embarrass her again. "Call the airline and return to Nassau with me."

She stood firmly beside her decision not to return with him.

John degraded himself to the point of begging.

But she would not hear of it. In fact, she tried to shake her wrist loose. Her struggle only caused him to grip her wrist more firmly.

She reared back and punched him in the mouth.

He loosened his grip on her wrist and looked at her for a second, running his hand across his mouth and wiping the blood from his lip. John froze like a statue. Funny, this same Johnny Reed would normally retaliate, woman or no woman.

At last, he conceded that he had lost the battle. He let it go. He turned and walked slowly toward the door, stopping only to stare at her one last time before leaving.

*   *   *

On his way home, John felt hungry. *Strange*, he thought, *"Why would I feel hungry after failing with Elaine. I should be down and out." Strange.*

He considered having lunch at the diner where his friend Lori the waitress worked, so he changed directions and headed for the diner.

Before entering, he realized that he had to arrange a return flight to Nassau.

Using the public phone located in the diner's vestibule, he called the airline.

A one o'clock flight was arranged for the next day.

When he entered the diner, Lori noticed him and pointed toward her designated work area. He sat at the far_____corner.

After taking his order, Lori asked, "How's everything?"

"Great, Lori. Just great. In fact I'm leaving for the Bahamas tomorrow for a couple of weeks."

"I'm happy, for you, John. Enjoy."

John thanked her. "Say, I'm free tonight. How about dinner, a show, and we'll top it off with my special night cap?" John asked, eyeing her up and down.

"I'll have to check my schedule first," she answered facetiously. John didn't say a word. He just stared at her.

"Okay, for you I'll cancel my appointment," she said with a smile.

John set the time for nine o'clock. "I'll rent a car today so you won't have to drive. Plus I'll be needing it for the airport."

With lunch finished, he placed a ten-dollar bill on the table. He left for the car rental agency.

Arriving home, he parked his rental car in his apartment's parking lot. John glanced at the truck he had brought back from Worthington and decided to get rid of the junker.

He picked up the keys and a screwdriver. He drove the truck to an isolated area and parked it in the midst of old factories. He removed the tag and then scratched over the repair shop address. He returned to his apartment, sat on the edge of his bed, and looked around the room. It suddenly occurred to John that his funds in the Bahamas needed to be replenished.

He stacked fifty thousand dollars neatly in a box, wrapped it, and placed it on the table. He planned to take it to the post office on his way to the airport the next day. He lay down to take a nap when Elaine entered his mind. Strangely, he no longer felt a desire for Elaine. John's mood could change from one minute to the next.

*   *   *

He awoke in time to dress and pick up Lori by nine o'clock.

They dined at Tony's restaurant. Afterward, they went to a local disco to listen to the latest sounds and danced the night away.

As John had promised, they ended the evening in bed with sex that lasted well into the dawn.

Fortunately for Lori, she did not have to report for work until one o'clock that afternoon.

John awoke first. He leaned toward the clock, which showed nine-thirty. He shook Lori awake. "What time is it John?" she asked.

"Get-out-of bed time," John answered.

Lori rested while John showered and shaved. It was her turn. She staggered to the bathroom for a shower and dressed while John packed his bags. He put the shoebox under his arm, took hold of his bags, and they left.

In the car, Lori heard someone calling, "Mr. Reed. Oh, Mr. Reed." She turned to John. "There's someone yelling for you."

John looked through the rearview mirror to see his apartment manager walking toward his car. He looked at his watch. "Fuck. I have no time for him. I have to get going." He started the engine, threw the car in gear, and sped away, the manager in hot pursuit, shouting for John to stop.

The manager finally stopped when he realized that John was not going to.

John drove Lori home and continued on to the post office with his parcel.

He arrived at the airport with little time to spare.

*   *   *

The return flight to Nassau was fast and smooth. Arriving at the hotel he was greeted by the hotel manager, who was happy to see John's return safely.

John thanked him and thought as he greased the manager's palm with a ten-dollar bill, *the same old bullshit, looking for the good old American dollar*.

John reminded him of the package that was due for him within the next day or two.

"No problem, sir," the manager answered.

John retired to his room.

He had just put his bag on the bed when the phone rang. He answered to hear Elaine's voice. She told him that she had had a change of mind and really loved him.

"I want to return to Nassau and be with you."

There was a pause before John asked, "Who's this?"

"Elaine. John, please!"

"I don't know anyone named Elaine. You must have the wrong number," John answered.

"John, please," she begged, again.

John didn't want to hear it. He slammed the receiver back in place.

You made your decision, bitch, he said to himself as he changed into his swimming trunks and went to the beach to bask in the sun.

*   *   *

In Chicago, Tony opened the restaurant for the day and was waiting for the kitchen help to check-in.

The chef was the first to arrive. He stopped to ask Tony if his friend John still lived in the apartment building on Swenson Street.

"Yes, so?" Tony asked.

"Well, I hope he knows that they are tearing down the building to replace it with a high-rise."

Tony jumped to his feet and bowled him over on his way to his car. He arrived in time to see the final blow of the huge iron ball crushing the last remaining rumbling wall.

He looked for and found the apartment manager who just happened to be standing close by. He rushed over to him, grabbed him by his lapels, and began shaking him.

"What the fuck's going on? Did you notify Mr. Reed that you were tearing the building down?" Tony was infuriated.

The manager was startled. "I'm ssssorry, sssssir. III dddon't understand. WWWe notifiedddd MMMMr. RRReed oooon numerous ooocasions."

Regaining his composure, Tony let go of the manager's lapels. After straightening his coat, the manager explained that all the residents were notified in writing, and he produced a sample flyer that had been placed under each apartment door every day for at least two weeks. He further explained that he saw John last week in his car.

"I yelled and tried to get his attention to tell him, but Mr. Reed wouldn't stop. In fact I chased his car for a block, but he completely ignored me." He further told Tony that John's furniture and belongings were shipped to a warehouse, and must be taken out of storage within ninety days, or the management would no longer be responsible. He furnished Tony the address of the warehouse.

Tony apologized and looked at the rubble. He shook his head as the huge dump trucks were hauling away the debris.

What a waste, all that fucking money, he thought.

He returned to his car and sped off to his restaurant.

Tony went directly to the phone to notify John.

"Sorry, sir, Mr. Reed does not answer."

"Tell him that Tony called and it's very important that he return my call as soon as possible."

The clerk saw the opportunity for a possible big tip from John, so he combed the beach and found him lying on the sand with a blonde. The clerk was correct. The search for John made him twenty dollars richer.

John wasted no time. In fact, he didn't even bother explaining to the blonde. He ran for the nearest phone and called Tony.

Tony asked him if he were sitting.

"I'm standing, Tony. What's up?"

Tony paused and then explained everything to John.

There was silence for what seemed to be an hour. Then John suddenly changed into Mr. Hyde. He began pounding the receiver against the wall, then pounding the receiver against the phone box and back onto the wall, cursing the world and all the people in it.

The phone receiver finally shattered to pieces. As if that were not sufficient, he tore the entire unit off the wall and tossed it wildly to the sidewalk. People in the vicinity scurried for cover.

Suddenly, John began laughing hysterically like a lunatic. His laughter stopped as abruptly as it had started. He placed his hands over his face, shook his head, and seemed to revert back to his calmer self.

He looked for and found another phone and called Tony.

He apologized to Tony. "I'm sorry for acting like an idiot."

"No need to apologize. I understand completely and would have reacted the same way."

"So that's what those fucking flyers were that I kept tossing in the trash without reading."

"You got it, John, and it cost you all that money."

John paused again.

"Well, Tony, it looks like lady luck has finally deserted me. What more could happen to fuck me up? It was wise that I mailed myself the fifty thousand dollars when I did. I should have sent the two hundred thousand that I originally thought of sending. Stupid fuck that I am."

Tony tried consoling him by telling him that at least he still had the restaurant business as a backup.

He thanked Tony, hung up the phone, and returned to the hotel bar and got plastered.

*   *   *

Chief Daniels notified Pat that Jackson's personal effects were still being held at the bank. They were unable to be delivered to his wife because she has been out of town visiting a sister. "Great, Chief. I'll meet you at the bank in morning." Pat paused and then asked the chief if it were possible for them to check out the crash site.

"No problem, Pat. I'll have all the information when you get here in the morning. Walking in and around the crash site, Pat turned to Daniels and said, "It's strange, mighty strange that there aren't any skid marks leading to the crash site, chief. Even someone who is dead drunk would try to stop a speeding car when realizing he was about to crash."

"Hmm, makes sense but . . ."

"Yeah, I know, chief. Well let's ride to the bank and see what we can uncover."

At the bank, Pat was going through the cardboard box. "Nothing of any value here, Chief." Pat suddenly had an idea. "Is there any chance that Jackson's vehicle is still in the area?"

"It was totaled, but let me check with the office." He called headquarters and was told that the vehicle was towed to a salvage yard. Daniels took the information, and he and Pat were off to the salvage yard. The car was still there, and Pat combed through as much as he could maneuver, since the car was crushed like a grape. Pat managed to go through the glove compartment and then the trunk. He then checked the storage pocket on the back seat. Finally Pat backed off and told Daniels that he was finished and it was time to return to the station.

*   *   *

John's package arrived, and he was immediately notified by the desk clerk.

He picked up his package and hurried to his room. He opened it and placed ten thousand dollars on the bed, afterwards hiding the balance in his usual place.

The next few days again found John enjoying his new life: eating, sleeping, gambling at the casino, and meeting young attractive women.

Suddenly, the women from the hotel, young and old, heard gossip that there was a handsome young bachelor who appeared to have lots of money. Wherever John was seen in the hotel lobby or hotel casino, the ladies swarmed around him like bees around honey.

After awhile, John realized that all the attention was beginning to get out of hand. He thought that he'd better start slowing down or someone other than the women would notice, especially the police. Even his parole officer might get wind of his extravagant living.

Coming to his senses, he took refuge at a secluded section of the beach. He even brought a lunch bag to the beach during the day and spent more time watching television.

Playing the lone ranger was working out fine. However, John being John could not abstain from sex very long. So he called Maureen, an airline hostess he had become acquainted with during his flights to and from Chicago, thinking that she might by chance be on the island between flights. Sure enough, she was there, so he arranged a meeting with her for dinner—but at her hotel for more privacy. She immediately agreed. While having dinner, she informed him that she was staying three additional days. "If you're interested."

He didn't have to think twice before answering, "You're on." The next two days found them on the beach in the morning and in bed between lunch and dinner. Nights found them dancing, gambling, and then back in bed having sex.

Maureen wanted to go to the beach early this day so that she could get a better tan before returning to Chicago. John agreed. She put on her bathing suit. John wore black shorts and a white pullover shirt. The sun was warmer than normal this particular morning. There wasn't even a sea breeze blowing. They spread a blanket on the sand, and John ordered drinks for the two of them. John removed his shirt, and he sat on the blanket. Maureen lay on the blanket on her stomach exposing her back to the sun. John was enjoying his drink while looking at the ocean and soaking up the warm sun when the wind began picking up. He felt a chill, and a sudden unease gripped him. He happened to turn to look in the direction of the hotel and noticed a well-dressed gentleman in a summer suit and tie walking toward him. John felt spooked. When the gentleman arrived, he said, "Good morning, Mr. Reed. You've been away from your hotel for a few days."

"You writing a book, Mr.?" John stared directly in his eyes.

"Reardon. Pat, please," Pat said sarcastically. Now John knew something was up, so he told Maureen to go back to the hotel and wait for him there. She hesitated and frowned. "NOW," John demanded. She picked up her belongings and walked back to the hotel. John looked at Pat and said, "Now, Mr. Reardon—Pat—or whatever your name is, what's your problem?"

Pat, without hesitating, replied, "I have no problem, Mr. Reed. You're the one with the problem."

"Okay, tell me what my problem is. Then get the fuck out of here."

For beginners, Pat flashed his card and picture identifying him as an FBI agent. He continued by asking John if he knew a George Jackson and if he were ever in Worthington, Ohio. "I never heard of either one," John answered.

"Oh, you were there all right, and I also know that you were involved with the bank robbery. I can't prove that, but I can prove you murdered George Jackson."

"Where did you get that stupid idea? From your Ouija board?" John laughed in Pat's face.

Pat grinned and took a small book from his inside coat pocket. "Do you know what this is, Mr. Reed?"

"Sure, it's a fucking book." John laughed again.

"No. Not an ordinary book, Mr. Reed. Or can I call you, John?"

"Look, I don't give a fuck what you call me. Now if you have something to tell me or show me, do it, or get the fuck out of my sight." John was becoming upset at this juncture. Pat ignored him, then raised the book in the air. "This, punk, is a diary and in case you don't know what a diary is, it's a log kept by people of the daily events in their lives." Now Pat was enraged as he continued.

"Jackson made an entry in this diary. I quote, 'I hope that this guy John Reed can be trusted, I'm taking one hell of a chance.'"

John looked up, directly into the sun. *Who would have thought that num-nuts Jackson would be smart enough to keep a fucking diary*, he thought to himself. John turned, looking back toward the hotel, and then turned his gaze back to Pat. Reardon stared back at John and said, "Don't even think about it, Mr. Reed. There are more FBI agents and local police lined up back there." John bent over to pick up his pullover shirt. As he did so, he scooped up a handful of sand in his left hand. He slowly stood up. He tossed the sand in Pat's face. He followed with two quick punches, one to the stomach and the other to the jaw. The impact of John's blows sent Reardon sprawling to the sand. John looked toward the hotel and then started running toward the ocean. He knew that it was his one and only chance to escape. Pat struggled to his feet; the other agents and local police were converging on the beach. Pat got up and sprinted after Reed, reaching for his 10mm as he ran. He shouted three warnings, and opened fire at John after the third warning. The other agents and police officers opened up on the fleeing murderer as the hot lead tore up patches of sand all around him. John fell on his face. He rolled to his right, then to his left, picking himself up before finally reaching the water. He began leaping over the waves. He fell a second time after more gunfire and finally, disappeared into the ocean. Pat and the agents ran into the ocean up to their waist. One of the agents tracking John through his binoculars shouted that he thought John was hit with a round, noticing dark spots on the back of John's shirt. "Possibly blood from a wound," one agent declared.

Dissatisfied with the agent's appraisal, Pat ordered them to stretch along the water's edge looking for anything that could possibly resemble a human body. After an hour of aerial and boat reconnaissance and beach patrol, the agents and local authorities could not find a trace of John Reed. The agents speculated that the suspect was probably taken out to sea by the rushing current. Reed was labeled, "Shark bait." Pat finally called off the search. He wouldn't treat Reed's fate so lightly. He ordered his men back to the hotel and released the local forces to their chief, thanking him for their invaluable assistance. When they were gone, he sat at the water's edge, looking and waiting for any movement. The agents standing at the hotel entrance shook their heads. They realized that Pat was obsessed with this case and that he would not accept the fact that John Reed was dead unless he found a body. Yet John had to have been hit by at least one bullet.

Finally, after four hours of sitting and the fall of darkness, Pat stood up. He turned and walked slowly back to the hotel and his room. He sat by the window overlooking the ocean, trying to convince himself that John Reed was indeed dead and that murderer had paid for his vicious crimes. But the uncertainty of an unconfirmed "knockdown" made the case incomplete, and in his mind, the book remained open on John Reed.